DEKOK AND THE CAREFUL KILLER

DeKok
and the
Careful Killer

by
BAANTJER

translated from the Dutch by H.G. Smittenaar

INTERCONTINENTAL PUBLISHING

ISBN 1 881164 07 1

Printing History:
    1st Dutch printing: October, 1976
    2nd Dutch printing: October, 1978
    3rd Dutch printing: April, 1979
    4th Dutch printing: June, 1980
    5th Dutch printing: October, 1981
    6th Dutch printing: January, 1984
    7th Dutch printing: July, 1985
    8th Dutch printing: December, 1987
    9th Dutch printing: May, 1989
    10th Dutch printing: July, 1990
    11th Dutch printing: August, 1990
    12th Dutch printing: November, 1990
    13th Dutch printing: February, 1991
    14th Dutch printing: October, 1991
    15th Dutch printing: March, 1992
    16th Dutch printing: December, 1992
    17th Dutch printing: June 1993

    1st American edition: 1993

Cover Photo: Peter Coene
Typography: Monica S. Rozier

DeKok
and the
Careful Killer

1

It was exactly twenty-seven minutes past midnight when Juliette Weer was found. She was in the middle of the pavement on her back in Slate Makers Alley, where the alley made a turn of almost ninety degrees. Her position was odd, cramped, with pulled-up knees twisted to one side and the hips to the other side as if she was trying to take up a lot less space than the alley provided. The single lamppost in the alley threw a yellow, diffused light on her pale face, wherein the bright red mouth was frozen into an expression of complete amazement.

Inspector DeKok of the ancient, well-known police station at Warmoes Street looked down on the corpse. His sharp gaze roamed from the blonde hair and the long, slender neck to the patent leather purse next to her shoulder. He pushed his old, decrepit little felt hat further back on his head and scratched behind an ear. Something bothered him, something jarred, did not fit in with the rest of the scene. He had seen hundreds of corpses in his long career with the Amsterdam Municipal Police. The years had made him sensitive to certain disturbances, deviations from the normal pattern.

Young Vledder, his assistant, friend and colleague, knelt down next to the head and aimed his flashlight at the neck of the victim.

"Strangled," he said tonelessly.

DeKok nodded slowly, his mind far away. The gray sleuth wrestled with his uneasy feelings. The sight of the woman mesmerized him, intrigued him. He could not tear his eyes away from the twisted corpse. His mind worked at top speed, combining, sorting, sifting, deducting, searching for the interfering dissonant in the shrill spectacle of violent death.

Vledder rose.

"What a shame," he said, shaking his head in commiseration. "Such a beautiful woman."

DeKok glanced at him.

"You mean she's too good looking to die so young?"

Vledder nodded sadly.

"Don't you agree?"

DeKok's face was distorted by a bitter grimace.

"The murderer didn't think so," he said, acid in his voice.

Vledder used a handkerchief to wipe the sweat from his forehead. He lacked the experience of his older colleague. Despite his brash appearance, a confrontation with death always shocked him, made his back run cold and his hands clammy. DeKok was probably the only person who knew about Vledder's inner turmoil in situations like this. To outsiders Vledder always appeared cool, calm, collected, unless he gave in to one of his precipitous, zealous, exuberant moods. Vledder had been known to submit the wildest theories in that state of mind.

"Murderers," said Vledder in an attempt to hide his feeling, "are a strange breed of people."

DeKok snorted.

"Seldom," he retorted. "In most cases they are frightfully unremarkable."

Bram Weelen, the police photographer, insinuated himself in between the two Inspectors.

"If you don't mind, I'd like to get at her to take my pictures. I don't exactly have all the time in the world, you know."

Vledder pointed at the dead woman.

"She does," he said.

It sounded laconic, but wasn't meant that way. Weelen looked at him for a few seconds and then turned to DeKok.

"He sounds more like you all the time," he growled.

DeKok looked sad.

"Yes, I've noticed that. But what do you expect. If you keep company with a wolf, you'll learn to howl."

Weelen decided to get on with his work. Once DeKok started spouting obscure adages, lectures would follow soon after.

"Any special requests?" he asked, readying his Hasselblad.

DeKok made a vague gesture.

"An overall shot, close-ups, the usual. But I would also like a shot of both entrances of the alley. Both going *out* and coming *in*. In other words from Old Front Fort Canal and from St. John Street."

"No problem. That all?"

"Yes, thank you."

Ben Kruger, the fingerprint expert was next. DeKok tapped him on the shoulder and pointed at the ground.

"I would like you to check the purse first. I want to know what's inside, but I want you to first check the outside for fingerprints."

Kruger smiled.

"I understand. But I don't have enough light here in the alley. Why don't I take it with me and deliver it to you at the station as soon as I'm through?"

"All right."

A large constable approached, holding a flashlight to light the way for Dr. Koning, the Coroner. DeKok met the old man half-way, stretched out his hand and greeted him heartily. He liked the eccentric old man in his old-fashioned clothes that seemed to have been bought in an earlier century. DeKok approved of old-fashioned things.

"A dead woman?" asked Dr. Koning in his peculiar, creaky voice.

DeKok nodded.

"We think it's strangulation," he said carefully. "There are signs of strangulation on the neck."

Dr. Koning laboriously lowered himself to his knees, lifted the eyelids of the corpse and aimed his flashlight at the pupils. He took a long time studying the marks in the neck. Then he rose slowly. DeKok hastened to help him to his feet. He peered at DeKok across his half-glasses that were precariously balanced on the tip of his nose.

"It's not all *that* clear," said the Coroner. "But it *does* look like strangulation with two hands. I think there are some marks on the side of the neck as well. Perhaps a scarf, or a necktie was used, it isn't impossible . . . But Dr. Rusteloos can probably give you more detailed information *after* the autopsy."

The old man hesitated, seemed momentarily confused. He looked around as if he was wondering how he had arrived in this narrow, stinking alley, wondered what he was doing there.

"By the way, Inspector," he said formally, "the woman is dead."

DeKok suppressed a smile.

"Thank you, doctor," he said just as formally. "Can you make a guess about the time of death?"

The Coroner raised both hands in a defensive gesture.

"No, no," he protested. "I would not care to be precipitous. Dr. Rusteloos should properly determine that. I would not want to hazard a guess at this time."

10

"Please, doctor," cajoled DeKok, suppressing another smile, well aware of the old man's peculiarities. "I won't hold you to it."

"Well, if you insist," capitulated Dr. Koning. "But this is with the clear understanding that it is off the record." He looked at DeKok with a stern face. DeKok readily nodded assent. "Well, in that case," continued the doctor, "in that case . . . I would say . . . roughly . . . three to six hours ago. But, please, do not depend on that. You really should wait for the results of the autopsy. You have enough surprises in your profession. Goodnight gentlemen."

He lifted his floppy, greenish Garibaldi hat in a courtly manner and left the alley in the wake of the unflappable constable.

Between shots, Bram Weelen managed to grimace at DeKok behind the Coroner's back.

Two attendants from the Coroner's office were waiting with the ubiquitous gurney. They kept out of the way, one hid a cigarette in the hollow of his hand, the other spat a long jet of tobacco juice at the disappearing tail of a passing rat. When the camera flashes stopped, they approached. They knew the routine. They glanced at DeKok who nodded permission. They placed the corpse in the body bag and the bag on the gurney. In silent cooperation, they passed the belts and buckles to each other and secured the bag. Their movements were quick, emotionless. They had seen too many corpses. One pulling, the other pushing, they took the body to the van that was left at the end of the alley. DeKok watched them leave.

Bram Weelen was putting his gear away.

"This very night I will lock myself in my darkroom," he mocked, "although I will thereby most certainly jeopardize my conjugal bliss."

DeKok grinned amiably.

11

"I'm sure that your conjugal arrangements can withstand this slight onslaught on its harmony." His tone changed and he turned toward Vledder. "Go with the corpse," he ordered, "and confiscate the clothes as soon as they have her laid out in the lab."

"Then what?"

"You *and* the clothes join me at the station."

"OK, Boss."

DeKok gave him a admonishing look. He liked his young colleague very much, but he definitely did not like to be addressed as "boss". That, coupled with "OK" was one of the few phrases that could really irritate him. He did not feel like a "boss" and did not want to be one. He had never pursued promotion and would probably refuse it in the unlikely event that it was ever offered to him. Rank did not have any attraction for him. He wanted to be what he was. Detective-Inspector, a hands-on cop with just enough rank and such an abundance of seniority that he never had to worry about being fired. That left him free to be a detective, a sleuth, a dealer in justice, at least, DeKok's own, peculiar brand of justice. His justice could not always be found in the law books. That did not necessarily make it less effective, or less just.

He took a last look at the spot where the dead woman had been, the acute angle of the alley, the single lamppost. Then he turned and walked slowly toward the end of the alley. He stopped at the corner of Old Front Fort Canal and watched the Coroner's van pick its way carefully along the narrow strip of pavement between the houses and the edge of the canal. Sometimes the wheels came very close to the water, because of the many bicycles that were piled against the facades of the buildings, two, sometimes three deep.

The other cars, the *Thundering Herd*, as DeKok called the small army of experts and specialists that always gathered around a violent death, had also left. A few curiosity seekers drifted slowly away into the bars and side streets, looking for the more exciting pleasures for which the Red Light District was famous.

Burying his hands deep in the pockets of his raincoat, DeKok walked back to the station house. His friendly, somewhat melancholy face, characterized by the deep creases of a friendly boxer, looked worried. He could not rid himself of a vague feeling that the death of the young woman was just the beginning. The possible start of a horrible series of murders that would demand the utmost of his knowledge and experience. He tried to identify the feeling, to examine it, but he did not succeed.

Small groups of "wise" guys and "bad" girls congregated on the corner of Old Church Square. Their assembly had something secretive, conspiratorial. The pimps hovered nervously on the outskirts of the small groups who whispered to each other in short, breathless sentences. The news of the murder had spread like wild fire. They fell silent as the Inspector passed.

Observing his surroundings with one part of his mind, DeKok walked on, apparently oblivious to the stealthy looks that were thrown in his direction. Fragments of music drifted from the bars and brothels. He picked up a piece of an inane melody about seamen's hearts and wide, deep seas. The repetitious, insistent music settled in his brain and chased away the chaotic thoughts about the dead woman. A group of drunken sailors stumbled from the *Old Sailors Place*, Sylvia's bar.

2

"Juliette Weer."

DeKok's eyebrows, which had often been suspected of living a life of their own, rippled across his forehead in a movement that defied every possible anatomical explanation. The movement could have been considered normal on an insect and then only if it was applied to that insect's antennae. On a human being it was totally inexplicable. Above DeKok's craggy, melancholy face, the effect had a tendency to make people catch their breath and question the evidence of their own eyes. Vledder, who was more familiar with the sight than most, nevertheless watched in spellbound fascination.

"Juliette Weer," repeated DeKok slowly. "It sounds familiar. I've heard that name before."

His features relaxed, his face assumed a thoughtful expression. Vledder shook himself, returned to the present. He tossed a passport on DeKok's desk.

"A certain Henry Weer was one of the big shots at C.I.H."

"Chemical Industry Holland?"

"Exactly. He died unexpectedly, about four or five months ago. It was in all the papers."

DeKok rubbed the bridge of his nose with a little finger.

"Yes," he responded slowly, hesitatingly. "I remember now. There was quite a hullabaloo about it. If I remember correctly, there were some papers that suggested that old man Weer did not die a natural death." He looked thoughtfully at Vledder. "Could she be a daughter?"

The younger man shrugged his shoulders.

"I don't know," he answered carelessly. "I haven't gone into family relations yet. I *do* know that the Weers belong to one of the richest families in Holland." He rubbed his nose in a subconscious imitation of DeKok's gesture. "And I think that Juliette, too, didn't have to watch the pennies. I figure that the chinchilla coat she wore would be more than my annual salary. The rest of her clothing as well . . . expensive stuff. You should see it."

"Later," waved DeKok. He picked up the passport and started to leaf through it. "Apparently she isn't married. At least there's no husband's name in the passport."

Vledder shook his head.

"Goes to show you," he said, "stupid guys. She's a beautiful woman. Almost a classical beauty." His voice trembled with admiration. "How old was she?" he asked.

"Let's see. Born in Wassenaar . . . that seems to indicate money . . . according to the latest statistics, there's more money in that little suburb of The Hague than anywhere else in Holland . . . oh, yes, her age . . . less than twenty-seven, barely twenty-six, actually. According to the passport she's five foot five, blue eyes and blonde hair. Her profession was analyst and she lived in Amsterdam."

He handed the passport back to Vledder.

"Tomorrow," he continued, "I'd like you to have the passport photo enlarged and have it circulated. It seems a recent photograph. According to the date on the passport, it was only issued last month. No visas, no exit, or entry stamps." He paused, rubbed his chin. "Were there any other papers in the purse?"

Vledder pointed vaguely into the direction of another part of the building.

"Ben Kruger is still working on it. You know how meticulous he can be."

DeKok grinned. At that moment the fingerprint expert entered the room. The first thing he saw was DeKok's grinning face. The somber features were lit up with boyish delight. A grinning DeKok was irresistible. Kruger's face was still red from the exertion of climbing the stairs in the old building, but a sunny smile broke through upon seeing DeKok's cheerful face. The expert threaded his way through the desks in the large, busy detective room and arrived in front of DeKok's desk. As DeKok's face changed from a happy grin to an expectant look, Kruger's smile disappeared to be replaced with an indignant expression. Tossing the purse on the desk, he lowered himself into a chair.

"You'd never believe it," he exclaimed disgustedly. "Nothing, absolutely nothing! Not even on the inside flap."

DeKok eyed him with surprise.

"Not even the fingerprints of the victim? They, at least, should be there."

Kruger shook his head.

"Everything has been wiped, wiped clean. Nothing, I mean nothing, has been left, not even a fragment. You may find this hard to believe, but even the mirror in her compact has been wiped clean."

"A careful killer."

"You can say that again. The perpetrator took his time. There's clear evidence of cool, calm deliberation."

DeKok sighed.

"Papers?"

17

The dactyloscopist gestured toward Vledder.

"I already gave him her passport. There was an empty envelope, no stamp, no cancellation, addressed to Ms. Juliette Weer, 237 Mirrors Canal, Amsterdam. The sender was simply identified as *Jonathan*."

"*Jonathan?*"

Kruger nodded.

"Just Jonathan. No surname, no address. I kept the envelope, because I want to try iodine vapors,* just in case. Otherwise I would have brought it with me. In any case, I'll be sure to send you a photocopy of the writing."

Vledder interrupted.

"What woman will keep an empty envelope in her purse with just her own address? For that matter, why would anybody keep such an envelope?"

DeKok pursed his lips.

"I think," he spoke carefully, "That the envelope *wasn't* empty. Our very careful killer must have taken off with the contents."

"You mean," asked Vledder, who sometimes had a talent for asking the obvious, "that the letter might have been incriminating?"

"Possibly. There are countless reasons why the letter could have been taken away. Perhaps the letter would have led directly to the murderer." DeKok had no trouble with the obvious, either.

Vledder gesticulated impatiently.

"But why take just the letter, why did he leave the envelope behind?"

DeKok shrugged his shoulders.

---

* In certain, special cases, fingerprints on paper may be revealed with the aid of iodine fumes.

"I think it's a bit soon to advance a reasonable theory for that. But you're right. It's passing strange. But let's stick to the facts for the moment." He turned toward Kruger. "Any money?"

"Certainly. A considerable amount, as a matter of fact. More than seven hundred in guilders and some coins in an antique, beaded change-purse. You better count it again at leisure. Also a folder with Traveller's Checks in dollars, a regular checkbook with a healthy balance and a number of gold credit cards. All in the name of J. Weer."

"Anything else?"

"No, the usual. Nothing special. Some jewelry, a gold watch, a diamond ring and a gold bracelet."

DeKok stood up and started to pace the narrow space between the desks. After several turns back and forth he paused.

"Well, at least we can rule out robbery," he said. "Apparently the killer wasn't after money."

Kruger stood up and disappeared in the direction of the door.

"I'm going home," he yawned. "Perhaps I can get a few hours sleep." He looked at DeKok and grimaced. "Murderers and their motives . . . that's your job. I'm glad I don't have to worry about that." Near the door he turned and waved. "Good luck, my friend," he shouted across the room, "you'll need it."

DeKok stared for a while at the door after it had closed behind Kruger.

"I should have become a fingerprint expert myself," he said wistfully.

Young Vledder came to stand next to him.

"They're all gone," he said bitterly. "The Coroner and his helpers, the photographer, Kruger, everybody. They're through. For them it's finished. We're just starting."

DeKok nodded slowly.

"And only God knows where it will lead."

19

It did not sound profane, but serious, almost mystical. He turned abruptly and sat down behind his desk. Vledder sat down on the edge of his own desk, a deep crease in his forehead as evidence of deep thoughts.

"You know, DeKok, this may sound crazy, but you know what was the first thing that came to mind when I saw her there under the lamppost?"

"Well?"

"What's a good-looking, well-dressed woman doing in that filthy Slate Makers Alley?"

DeKok slid further down in his chair.

"I don't think," he hesitated, "that she even saw the alley."

"What?"

DeKok shook his head.

"No," he said sadly. "She's never been there . . . alive."

Vledder looked confused.

"What *do* you mean?"

The face of the old Inspector became expressionless, a mask.

"Juliette Weer didn't die in that alley . . . she was put there."

Vledder gaped at him.

"Put there?" there was disbelief in his voice. "Whatever makes you say that?"

DeKok smiled gently.

"A simple observation of the facts," he chided gently. "And a good insight. Believe me, if you had paid attention, you would have come to the same conclusion."

Vledder looked insulted.

"What facts?"

DeKok leaned forward, rested his elbows on the edge of the desk and rested his chin in his folded hands.

"I don't blame you," he soothed. "On the contrary. But from the very first moment I had a feeling that something didn't fit." He smiled. "Didn't compute, as you're so fond of saying. Anyway, I felt there was something wrong with the overall picture. I racked my brains, but I just couldn't put my finger on it. It took me a while before I realized what was wrong."

He rummaged through his pockets and found a piece of hard candy. He contemplated it for a while. Then he continued.

"You see," he said while he carefully peeled the wrapper from the candy, "those bent knees bothered me. They did not fit in with the rest of the scene. If somebody dies on his, or her, back and there's room, the legs will stretch. The muscles relax and the weight of the legs is enough to stretch them." He sighed as he removed the last sliver of paper from the candy. The sweet must have been in his pocket a long time, because the paper seemed to have melted to the outside of the confection. He contemplated it for a few seconds and then popped it in his mouth.

"Juliette Weer was found on her back," he continued. "When they put her in the body bag, I noticed that the limbs had frozen in that position. Rigor mortis normally sets in about an hour or so after death and usually starts in the jaw. After three to six hours the entire body is frozen into position. Please note . . . that's frozen in the position in which the body finds itself at the time."

"And that means," completed Vledder, "that Juliette was dead when she arrived in the alley and that rigor mortis had already set in."

DeKok raised a forefinger in the air.

"Excellent, really excellent," he said. "From that we conclude that she died three to six hours *before* she was placed in the alley. She died with pulled up knees."

Vledder needed no further prodding.

"Sitting down," he exclaimed. "She died, at least, *froze*, into position after she died, while she was sitting in a chair. And," he added, "as I remember the position of her knees, it must have been a low chair."

"Yes," admitted DeKok, " a low chair, or . . . the back seat of a car."

They remained silent. As happens so often, it seemed that everybody else in the room was silent at the same time. For several minutes an eerie hush descended on the usually so busy and raucous detective room. A drunk could be heard clearly in the street below as he tried to murder an unidentifiable song.

Vledder was the first to break the silence. As if waiting for a signal, the low hum of voices resumed and Vledder and DeKok were again insulated in their own private capsule of background noise.

"You know, DeKok," he said glumly, "there was at least one who *did* know all about Slate Makers Alley . . . the killer."

DeKok did not react. From time to time he had the annoying habit of being able to ignore everything and everybody with a sublime indifference. It seemed as if he had not heard Vledder's words. Vledder, well attuned to DeKok's moods and habits, waited patiently.

Minutes went by. Then DeKok started to move. He seemed to be moving in slow motion, but before Vledder had realized it, he had gone over to the coat rack, grabbed his old, decrepit little hat and was already halfway to the door when he tossed a remark over his shoulder.

"Bring her keys," he told Vledder.

Vledder looked after the fast disappearing figure of DeKok.

"What keys?" he shouted.

Impatiently, DeKok halted in mid-stride, turned around and pointed at his desk.

"The keys from her purse," he said in a raised voice. "We're going to the Mirrors Canal."

3

The night was sultry. The warmth of the day lingered and stuck to the asphalt and the facades of the old canal houses. The water in the canals had the appearance of luke-warm soup. The Red Light District had slowed down because of the heat, but did not sleep. No matter what the hour of the day, or the night, there were always people in the streets and along the canals and, of course, behind the windows of the brothels and the single rooms that formed the "office" spaces of the thousands of prostitutes. The district encompassed the old inner city of Amsterdam, a veritable labyrinth of narrow streets, small canals, quaint old bridges, dark alleys, unexpected squares and architectural wonders. All enlivened by exotic, often beautiful ladies, well-dressed pimps, innumerable bars and eating establishments of every kind. The endless streams of the sexually deprived, or those who thought they were and, of course, the bus loads of tourists from all over the world and the seamen from every nationality mixed with the locals of the centuries old Quarter to create an atmosphere which could not be duplicated anywhere else in the world. It was not as if the crimes and vices that existed in the Quarter could not be found anywhere else in the world. No, the crucial difference was created by the remarkable tolerance of the Dutch. Almost any desire could be indulged in the district and seldom, if ever, would the gratification of those desires raise so much as an eyebrow. Vice was a business and the participants made every effort to keep it "clean".

Nevertheless, it made the old, renowned police station at Warmoes Street, situated at the edge of the Red Light District, the busiest police station in Northern Europe. The hundreds of thousands of visitors to the Quarter created their own problems, and opportunities. Crime ranged from spiked, or watered drinks with the resultant bar fights to having one's pockets picked by a prostitute; from an "ordinary" mugging to murder. But the station did not have a vice-squad.

All this went through DeKok's mind as Vledder reached the Prince's Canal and parked the car. The engine still "dieseled" a bit as DeKok hoisted himself out of his side of the car and Vledder scrambled to follow him. Vledder kicked one of the fenders of the old VW Beetle.

"Have you ever seen the limousines American cops have?" he asked. "They'd probably use this car for target practice. It's a disgrace."

DeKok smiled indifferently. Cars did not interest him. They were mechanical, something modern. They had to be endured. His favorite mode of locomotion consisted of his own two feet. Sometimes he envied the few remaining beat-cops who still patrolled on foot. They were not insulated from the public by steel and glass, they could approach people on human terms. Like most good cops, DeKok genuinely liked people. Both occupied with their own thoughts, they crossed the bridge that brought them to the uneven-numbered side of the Mirrors Canal. They stopped in front of 237 and looked up. No lights were visible. A yellow brass plate on the shiny, lacquered door announced *J. Weer* in discreet black letters.

DeKok pushed the bell. They could hear the noise outside. But nothing happened. The house remained silent. The canal

26

looked placid in the moonlight and the houses dozed on, undisturbed by their earlier footsteps and the ringing of the bell.

After a few minutes, DeKok looked left and right along the row of houses, then he produced the keys from the handbag and unlocked the front door. They took another, quick look around. They saw nobody . . . nobody was in sight. Vledder pushed the door farther and both men entered. Carefully, following the beams of their flashlight, they entered the hall. There they stopped and listened. Not a sound could be heard. The house seemed deserted. A grandfather clock slowly ticked away the seconds.

They were facing a long, marble corridor. Carefully they proceeded. The corridor led to a modern kitchen in the back of the house. DeKok looked around, felt the pots and pans, looked at the stove and rubbed his finger over the surface. He opened the refrigerator. The interior light created bizarre shadows on the walls and the ceiling.

"Hungry?" grinned Vledder.

DeKok did not answer. He left the kitchen and went back into the corridor. Halfway down he opened a door and entered a large sitting room with a high ceiling. He walked over to the windows. Heavy, red curtains had been closed tightly.

Turning around, he aimed the beam of his flashlight through the room. The oval light danced across a black marble mantelpiece, an old-fashioned pendulum, a leather sofa, deep, comfortable chairs and a table formed by a slab of onyx, supported by intricately wrought iron. He went over to the sofa and inspected it minutely. Then he knelt down and touched the carpet with exploring fingers.

Vledder looked down on him.

"What are you looking for?"

"A wet spot."

"What?"

DeKok rose.

"A wet spot," he repeated. "Juliette Weer died of strangulation, or so we assume. Remember?" There was a sarcastic undertone to the voice.

Vledder bit his lower lip and nodded.

"Of course," he said, "and in case of strangulation, most victims empty their bladder."

He spoke as if by rote, a bit mockingly but with a hint of irritation. He was annoyed with himself for having overlooked such an obvious possibility. As usual, DeKok was right. It was entirely possible that Juliette had been killed in her own home and later, in an effort to create a diversion, had been transported to the filthy Slate Makers Alley. With renewed interest he looked around.

"I see no signs of a struggle."

DeKok shook his head, darting the flashlight beam here and there.

"It's not necessary. Perhaps she did not have the chance to resist. If the strangler knew what he was about . . ."

He halted in mid-sentence. Outside, on the quiet canal could be heard the shrieking, whining sound of braking tires, immediately followed by the slamming of a car door. Inspector DeKok slinked over to the windows and peered between the curtains. He saw a man approach the house with quick steps.

"Put off your light," he whispered, "someone is coming."

They could hear the lock click in the hall. The corridor light flashed on and the light leaked across the threshold of the door. The two cops stood next to each other, straining to hear every sound. They heard the door slam shut, followed by the sound of careful, cautious footsteps. Vledder and DeKok separated and placed themselves on either side of the door. Vledder had his pistol ready. They saw the shadow of the visitor's feet in the light that spilled over underneath the door. The visitor hesitated, as if aware of an unnamed danger.

The doorknob turned slowly. The door opened and a broad beam of light slid across the room. For just a moment the silhouette of a man was visible against the light in the corridor. Then the entire room was lit up as DeKok threw the switch.

The visitor looked shocked at the sudden appearance of DeKok in front of him. DeKok stretched out a hand.

"How do you do?" he asked politely. "My name is DeKok, with kay-oh-kay."

The man swallowed.

"DeKok?" he repeated, stunned.

"Yes. And if you'll make a quarter turn to the right, you'll meet my partner, Inspector Vledder."

The man turned, looked confused and seemed to blanch under the withering look from the young Inspector.

"W-what, . . . eh, w-what do you want? What are you doing here?" he stammered.

DeKok did not answer, but cocked his head slightly and studied the visitor intently. He saw a man in his early forties, tall, slender, handsome, with large, brown eyes and wavy, black hair with a light graying at the temples.

"Who let you in?" asked the man. His tone had become more firm.

DeKok's eyebrows rippled briefly. The man stared in stunned disbelief, speechless. It was the most unexpected reply to his question. Then, as DeKok's forehead returned to normal, he seemed to hear DeKok's statement for the first time.

"I don't remember," taunted DeKok, "that you introduced yourself, Mr. . . . . eh?"

The man stuck out his chin.

"Bearburgh . . . Andrew Bearburgh. I'm a friend . . . a good friend of Juliette."

29

DeKok smiled an ingratiating smile.

"I understand. An intimate friend, intimate enough to have a key to the house."

Andrew Bearburgh gestured gracefully.

"It's an old privilege," he said simply. "It has never been withdrawn. After all, I *was* married to her for more than five years."

DeKok nodded with a fatherly gesture inviting further confidences.

"Five years," he said pensively. "And your relationship with your ex-wife is still so intimate that you can permit yourself to visit her in the middle of the night." He paused. "Unannounced," he added and then, with a complete change in his tone of voice: "Are you still checking up on her?"

"Checking up?"

"Yes. I don't recall you ringing the bell. Was it intended to be a surprise check?"

Andrew's face became red.

"We're legally divorced," he shouted angrily. "Juliette is free to come and go as she pleases. I don't check up on her."

DeKok's face assumed an expression of utter incredulity.

"Not checking up?" The surprise in his voice matched the expression on his face. "What other reason could you have? How do you intend to explain your visit at this time of night?"

Bearburgh shook his head as if trying to clear it. He was speechless. His mouth fell open and he looked stupefied.

"Explain? Explain?" he managed to utter, finally.

DeKok gave him a friendly, encouraging nod.

"I'm waiting," he said laconically. "What are you doing here?"

The man stared at him, thunderstruck. Then something seemed to snap inside him, something seemed to break the last restraints of self-control. He gesticulated wildly. His dark eyes flashed angrily.

"That's none of your damned business," he screamed. "I don't have to explain myself to you. I don't have to tell you a thing. NOTHING, you hear me? What gives *you* the right to come in here and ask me questions? How dare you. I want you to leave, right now!"

He pointed at the door with a dramatic, imperious gesture.

DeKok watched him carefully, his gaze never wavered from the man's face. He took it all in and stored it for future review.

"I will only leave," he said slowly, "at the express request of the occupant."

Andrew Bearburgh pressed his lips together, looked from Vledder to DeKok and back again.

"All right," he said vehemently. "If that's the way you want it, I'll ask her to tell you to leave. Is she up there?" He pointed toward the upper floor.

"Who?"

"Juliette."

DeKok did not answer immediately. He pushed his lower lip forward and shrugged his shoulders.

"I don't know if she's up there," he said seriously, looking for words, "that . . . that's not for me to know."

Andrew looked closely at the Inspector. There was something in DeKok's voice that made him uneasy.

"What are you trying to say?" he asked uncertainly.

DeKok sighed.

"Juliette Weer," he said resignedly, "is not . . . is no longer among the living. She was murdered a few hours ago."

It took several seconds before DeKok's words penetrated. Then he clapped his hands to his head. He paled.

"Murdered?" he asked hoarsely.

DeKok nodded.

"Strangled."

Andrew Bearburgh swayed on his feet. His groping hand clawed for support from the doorpost.

"After all," he whispered.

DeKok pounced on the remark.

"What do you mean?"

"For weeks I've seen it coming."

"The murder?"

Bearburgh nodded.

"Something like that. One cannot play games with other people's lives. Sooner or later you will be punished. I warned her. Time and time again. But she just wouldn't listen." He laughed without merriment, a short, barking, bitter laugh. "She really believed that all men were as easy-going as I."

DeKok looked him full in the face.

"You're easy-going?"

"To the point of madness."

"But you're divorced."

"Because she wanted a divorce. She wanted her *freedom*." He pronounced the word as if it was a curse. Again he voiced the strange, bitter laugh. "Freedom! She had dozens of affairs while we were still married. Openly, she made no secret of it."

"She was unfaithful."

"She was shameless. She never tried to hide her affairs, even from me. After the divorce she really let go. Everybody talked about it."

DeKok looked intrigued.

"At that point," he asked, "why would you care?"

Andrew Bearburgh lowered himself into a chair. His face had regained some color.

"I loved her," he said tonelessly. He looked at the older man. "Love doesn't stop when the lawyer calls you to tell you

you're divorced. Love remains. You refuse to believe that everything that went before is now gone ... extinguished." He shook his head in despair. "As if it never happened." It sounded cynical, but DeKok heard the anguish. He sat down across from the man.

"So, the divorce didn't mean a thing to you," he said softly. "You no longer lived at the same address, but that was all. Your feelings had not changed. You kept checking up on her."

Andrew looked up suddenly.

"I did *not* check up on her," he said sharply.

DeKok nodded calmly.

"You said that before," he said quietly. "But you were not surprised about her sudden death. You had, more or less, expected it." He leaned closer to Juliette's ex-husband. His eyes seemed to bore into the man's skull.

"Andrew Bearburgh," he asked in a compelling tone of voice, "who was less easy going ... less tolerant than you?"

4

A steady rain had washed the dirt and grime from the rooftops and streets and had wrapped the busy traffic into a barely penetrable veil of water and evaporating mist. The trees dripped and the age-old facades leaned against each other as if seeking shelter from the elements and comfort in each other's presence while contemplating their images in the shiny road surfaces. Amsterdam has an undeniable charm, especially when it rains.

Detective-Inspector DeKok stood in front of the window in the office of Commissaris* Buitendam and looked out over the rooftops. From his vantage point he could just see a part of the Dam, the large square in front of the Central Station, the departure point for the many sightseeing boats that criss-crossed Amsterdam's ancient canals. Despite the rain, the boats were full and a steady stream of eager customers waited their turn. Rain had never stopped the Dutch. Tourists seemed to adapt rapidly. They came in droves from all over the world. Those from wet places, such as Oregon and the Pacific Northwest, felt a familiar touch of home and those from arid places marvelled at the wonder of it all. Those from high places might experience a twinge of uneasiness when they realized that all this water was coming down on a country that was already below sea-level. But

---

* Commissaris, a rank equivalent to Captain.

on they came. They came for the tulip bulbs and the windmills. But also for the canals and stately homes of Amsterdam, the harbors and the Criers Tower, the Rijks Museum with its magnificent collection of Rembrandts. They came to see the birthplace of Peter Stuyvesant and Vincent van Gogh and the old church in Leiden where the Pilgrims worshipped before they sailed on the Mayflower. And a good many came for the Red Light District.

DeKok bounced up and down on the balls of his feet and enjoyed the view. He loved Amsterdam, *his* Amsterdam, the old inner city where he knew every street, every alley, every bar and almost every person. Those he did not know, knew him.

Behind him the Commissaris orated. The tall, stately Chief of the Warmoes Street station paced up and down. His cultured voice sounded high, nervous, a bit hurried. He scraped his throat a lot.

"DeKok," he said, agitated, "we *have* to do something about this. I mean, we can hardly treat this murder . . . routinely. The Weer family is *very* influential. Only this morning I had to speak to the Judge-Advocate. He called me personally. Mr. Overcinge expects rapid results. He, too, has been approached by a number of people. Apparently he is experiencing pressure from above. Juliette Weer was very much loved in certain circles. She had important friends."

"Also in Heaven?"

The Commissaris stopped in mid-stride and looked at the back of his subordinate.

"That is . . . that's an indecent remark," he said sharply. "Absolutely uncalled for."

DeKok turned around slowly. The commissarial outburst had not upset him in the least. He waved a hand through the air, as if brushing away a fly.

"What good are Juliette's earthly friends now?" There was irony in his voice. "All they can do is pray for her."

The Commissaris came closer. Red blushes tinged his pale cheeks.

"I don't care about Heaven," he shouted. "Whether you like it or not, you're an *earthly* detective and I'm a damned *earthly* commissaris. And the *earthly* friends of Juliette Weer can cause us a lot of trouble!"

DeKok looked at him evenly.

"And?" It sounded like a challenge.

Commissaris Buitendam reacted angrily.

"I want no trouble . . . not with anybody. Understand?"

DeKok moved away from the window. He understood his boss very well. The old man was close to his pension and had little appetite for complications with higher-ups.

He stopped in front of his Chief.

"I *will* find Juliette's killer," he said slowly, emphasizing the words. "Not because I want to do you a favor . . . not because the lady had important friends . . . most certainly not because of the Judge-Advocate and all those behind *him*, but because murder is an extremely unsympathetic way to end a discussion."

He ambled leisurely toward the door. For a moment the Commissaris gaped after his retreating figure. Then he realized what DeKok had just said.

"OUT!" he roared.

Like Vledder, the Commissaris would sometimes make superfluous remarks.

* * *

Vledder gave DeKok an amused look. He well knew how the conversations between his friend and their Chief usually ended.

"Did the boss have anything new to say?" he grinned.

DeKok searched his pockets and found a candy-bar. The wrapper and the contents had become a solid mess. With nonchalant ease he sailed it across the room and into a waste basket.

"Juliette had friends," he said with obvious annoyance. "They're putting pressure on all and sundry to quickly find her killer."

"What kind of friends?"

DeKok shrugged his shoulders.

"I don't know. In any case, they're important enough to put pressure on the Judge-Advocate. The Commissaris seemed flustered by it all."

Vledder's face cleared.

"O-h-o," he stretched with a knowing look. "In that case I can tell you which way the wind blows. You see, Juliette is indeed the daughter of old Henry Weer."

"From Chemical Industry Holland."

"Yes, mighty CIH, the State's showcase with a Board of Directors consisting almost exclusively of former, high-ranking government officials."

DeKok whistled between his teeth. A sound that made one think of chalk on a blackboard.

"So that's what's bothering them. The Commissaris is afraid we'll uncover a hornet's nest." His search finally led him to his breast pocket. With a gesture of triumph he discovered a toffee. "And old Henry's death is still as much of a mystery as before?"

Vledder nodded.

"Yes, I checked. According to the official report he died of a heart attack. But rumors, creditable rumors, persist that he was poisoned."

"Poisoned?"

"Aboard his yacht *Julia*. On that day there was a business conference on board, including most of the outside directors of the company. Then there was a sort of family reunion in the evening. All members of the clan were present. Henry retired momentarily after dinner. About half an hour later they found him dead in his cabin."

"Who found him?"

"Juliette."

DeKok put the toffee in his mouth and flicked the balled-up wrapper into an empty ashtray.

"Was there an investigation?"

Vledder shook his head.

"No, no investigation. No police investigation, I mean. After Henry had been found, the family decided unanimously to call Dr. Gelder. Dr. Gelder is the family physician. You know how that goes. He brought most of the little Weers into the world. An old, trusted family retainer. He came at once, looked at the corpse and wrote out a Death Certificate on the spot."

"Cause of death: heart attack?"

"Exactly. Just another natural death." Vledder sketched an incomprehensible symbol in the air. "There was no need for a police investigation after that."

DeKok nodded understanding.

"And old Henry's complete corpse was subsequently buried with full honors."

"What do you mean?"

DeKok smiled.

"Intact. No autopsy. No way to determine if he had been poisoned."

Vledder stretched his arms wide.

"What do you want? That's what the family wanted. No scandal."

DeKok pulled his lower lip forward and let it plop back. He repeated the annoying gesture several times.

"How did the rumor get out? I mean, where was the leak? Who started the rumor?"

"A member of the crew. A few days after the funeral a certain Johan Peter Opperman, able seaman, native of Horn, reported to one of the newspapers and uttered the suspicion that Henry Weer had *not* died a natural death. The seaman opined that the old man had been poisoned during the dinner."

"Was it a *reasonable* suspicion?"

"I don't know, it was never clarified."

DeKok's face, which had become placid under the soothing influence of the toffee, became annoyed all over again.

"Why did he go to the newspaper, rather than the police?"

Vledder shrugged.

"I read the article. According to the seaman he had expected a full-blown police investigation. When that didn't happen, he decided to make public what he knew."

"Well, was there an investigation after that?"

"No, at least not what you would call an investigation. A report was published."

"Who?"

"The State police, or the detective branch of the State police. I'm not exactly sure. *Julia* was in the port of Horn at the time of old Henry's demise. I don't know who was finally instructed to follow-up. In any case, based on the report, the provincial Judge-Advocate in Alkmaar decided that no further investigation was warranted."

DeKok rubbed his face with both hands, ruffled his hair and finally placed both hands in the back of his neck. He leaned further back in his chair.

"I understand," he said at length. "He didn't have enough to go on. Also, a further investigation would inevitably have led

40

to exhumation of the body. And that would have created a furor, locally *and* internationally. The Judge-Advocate over there probably was afraid to open a can of worms on the single, solitary say-so from a seaman." He paused. Then he suddenly brought his chair forward and leaned both elbows on the desk. "Still," he continued, "I wouldn't mind asking Opperman a few questions."

Vledder looked at him.

"That would be rather difficult."

"How's that?"

"Two days after his press interview, he fell overboard during a storm in the North Sea and drowned."

"That was before the police had talked to him?"

"Yes."

"What about the body?"

"It was never found."

They remained silent. It was a strange, pregnant silence. Their faces became even, expressionless. It was as if both men were suddenly aware of a threatening danger that seemed about to engulf them.

DeKok finally rose heavily from his chair.

"An unsavory business," he said solemnly. "And the question remains as to how much Juliette's death has to do with it all, if anything. Perhaps both cases stand alone."

He rubbed his eyes with a tired gesture. He stood for a while, as if undecided, knowing he was expressing a hope that was almost certain to be dashed. There had to be a connection between the two deaths. He looked at Vledder.

"Found out anything about Juliette's non-tolerant friend?"

The young Inspector studied his notes.

"According to reliable information, he's Mr. William O. Summerfield, a young, intrepid attache at the American Embassy."

"And?"

Vledder sighed.

"Toward the end of last week he was transferred to Athens."

DeKok smiled wanly.

"Athens," he repeated. "That's a long way off. It's hardly to be expected that the brash young suitor flew back just to kill his unfaithful mistress."

Vledder shook his head, flipping pages in his notebook.

"That didn't happen. He's in the clear. According to most reliable information, Mr. Summerfield has not left Athens since his arrival. On top of that, the love between Mr. Summerfield and our Juliette had cooled down considerably. For some time Mr. Summerfield has had a liaison with a classical Greek beauty. His transfer was at his own request."

DeKok's eyebrows rippled briefly then subsided just as quickly. For once Vledder missed the display. He was still staring at his notebook.

"Well," said DeKok, "in that case there's something wrong with the statements of Andrew Bearburgh. I was afraid of that."

Vledder looked up, surprise on his face.

"Did I miss something?" he asked.

DeKok grinned broadly.

"He, himself, was with Juliette last night. They had dinner together. She left the Amstel Hotel around eight o'clock last night."

Vledder swallowed.

"That . . . that's . . . "

DeKok nodded complacently.

". . . That's very close to the time of death," he completed.

5

Vledder looked at DeKok in surprise.

"How do you know that?"

"Know what?"

"That Andrew had dinner with Juliette shortly before she died. He didn't say a thing about that."

DeKok turned toward Vledder.

"Do I ask you," he said petulantly, "how you found out all those details about Old Henry and Mr. William O. Summerfield?"

Vledder pointed at the telephone on his desk.

"Ah, but that's easy. I just called here and there and of course it helps that I have a friend at the American Embassy."

DeKok smiled.

"My information isn't all that mysterious either," he said in a friendly tone of voice. "When we left the Mirrors Canal yesterday, I took a good look at Andrew's car. It's an unusual car. A light-blue Opel of a new model, with headlights that disappear when not in use and a lot of other fancy stuff. It reminded me of that American car, the Convair, Corvair, something . . ."

It was Vledder's turn to smile.

"A Convair is, was an airplane," he interrupted. "And don't let anybody hear you confuse a Corvair with a Corvette. One is something of a dirty word in automotive circles and the other is indeed a sleek, racing type car. The Corvette is probably one of the best cars ever built and . . ."

He stopped when DeKok raised his hand in protest. Vledder was picking up steam and in danger of becoming entirely too technical for DeKok's liking.

"Whatever," said DeKok. "I took down the number and asked the Communications Room to inquire if anybody had seen the car. It *was* an unusual automobile."

Vledder smiled to himself. Of course, DeKok would have asked someone else to send the request. DeKok would do almost anything to avoid using such modern communication methods as a fax machine. He had been known to barely tolerate the old-fashioned telex messages in the not-too-distant past. Vledder always felt that Dr. Koning and DeKok would have made a great pair . . . some two hundred years ago. Dr. Koning looked like he lived in the past, but DeKok longed for the past. It was always a marvel to Vledder, and others, how DeKok with his well-known abhorrence of modern life managed to be so competent as a policeman.

Unaware of Vledder's indulgent thoughts, DeKok continued.

"This morning, before I saw the Commissaris, I was contacted by a motorcycle cop. He had seen the car on Tulip Square, in front of the Amstel Hotel. He had stopped to, in his own words, 'take a closer look at that jewel' and that was all there was to it."

Vledder smiled openly.

"And then you forced yourself to phone the *Amstel* and talked to the *maitre d*'." He nodded wisely. "I bet you even know what they had for dinner."

DeKok laughed out loud.

"Exactly. I do." Suddenly he looked at the clock on the wall of the detective room. "Make sure you're in time for the autopsy. I don't want Dr. Rusteloos to have to wait for you." He walked over to the coat rack and struggled into his raincoat. "Ask him to keep something aside for a toxicological investigation."

Vledder could not hide his surprise.

"But she was strangled! What do you want with toxicology?"

"Juliette was aboard *Julia* when old Henry died. As long as I don't know for certain what happened there, how, what and if poison was used, I'd rather be safe than sorry. No sense in taking chances. Some poisons take a long time to dissipate in the body."

Vledder emerged from behind his desk.

"There's no indication that the other family members ingested poison."

"True. But there are also no indications that it *didn't* happen. Keep Johan Peter Opperman in mind, please. He spoke about poisoning during dinner. We don't know if it was a guess, or a fact. Sometimes the effect of poison is determined by the resistance to, the sensitivity for a particular poison that has been administered. How sensitive was old Henry Weer?"

Vledder stared at him.

"It's not at all unlikely," continued DeKok, "that Juliette and the other family members ingested the same amount of poison, but that Henry was the only one to succumb."

Vledder's quick mind recovered from his initial surprise and he nodded thoughtfully.

"In that case the poisoner must have known that Henry had less resistance to that particular poison than the others."

"If he was the objective."

"You lost me."

DeKok gestured, encompassing the room.

45

"We don't know who the killer, if there was a killer, was after. The target could have been another family member, or the whole family."

Vledder shrugged resignedly.

"In any case, you want to look for a connection between Henry's death and that of Juliette."

DeKok sighed.

"I don't know," he said. His voice sounded hesitant, unsure. "Everything is still a bit vague, nebulous is the word. There's no obvious connection. But I have a feeling about this ... there's a connecting link somewhere, somehow. Two members of the Weer family died within six months of each other. One is *rumored* to be poisoned and the other almost certainly died elsewhere than where she was found."

He stopped. His thoughts were far away while he stared at nothing in particular. His lips narrowed into a thin line. A stubborn look came over his face. Vledder knew the signs. DeKok considered the two deaths a personal affront. He would not rest until he had solved all the riddles surrounding the death of Henry Weer and until he had found the man who had wrapped his hands around the slender neck of Juliette Weer.

After a while DeKok's face relaxed.

"Please convey my heartiest greetings and respects to Dr. Rusteloos," he said as he placed his old, felt hat firmly on his head.

Vledder followed him.

"Where are *you* going?"

DeKok turned around and there was no mistaking the naughty gleam in his eyes. There was no other way to describe it.

"Little Lowee's. Only the velvet touch of a venerable cognac can slake the thirst that burns within me."

* * *

Lowee, who was called "Little" for obvious reasons, spread a friendly smile on his mousy face, abandoned the rinsing of glasses, wiped his fingers on the towel he wore around his waist and stretched out his hand to DeKok.

"Welcome in my establishment . . . as always."

DeKok hoisted his heavy body on a barstool.

"And a good afternoon to you," he replied.

"Same recipe?"

Without waiting for an answer, the small barkeeper reached under the counter, produced a bottle of Napoleon cognac and placed it with a reverent gesture in front of the Inspector.

"One of the last of my old supply," he whispered happily.

With practiced ease he placed two large snifters next to the bottle and then he poured the golden liquid into the glasses with a solemn, respectful movement.

Detective-Inspector DeKok watched with a satisfied smile on his face and an expectant look in his eyes. He loved these moments. Despite Lowee's checkered past and, to be honest, his far from blameless present, DeKok could not help but like the small, street-wise barkeeper. He was DeKok's kind of crook, the kind that broke the law, but was not vicious, not mean, and was always ready to help those who needed help. Lowee was an old-fashioned sort of criminal. So different from the violent, often drug-addicted criminals who were becoming more and more prevalent all the time. Even crime is going to hell, thought DeKok.

"*Proost*."

DeKok lifted the glass and slowly rocked it in his hand while he concentrated on inhaling the delicious bouquet that wafted up to his nostrils. Carefully he took his first sip. Slowly and smoothly the soothing liquid slid past his gullet. He took another look at the glass and replaced it on the counter with a tender touch.

"Some things," he philosophized, "can reconcile you to almost anything."

Lowee laughed.

"You guys busy?"

DeKok shrugged his shoulders.

"Never a recession in crime," he dodged.

Lowee took another swallow.

"You got anything to do with the dead dame in Slate Makers Alley?"

DeKok grinned softly. Lowee almost always knew what was going on in the Quarter.

"You have a hint for me?" he mocked.

The little barkeeper looked at him.

"Get real, DeKok," he said.

DeKok became aware of Lowee's serious tone but he merely placed his little hat a bit further back on his head and took a long swallow from his cognac.

"I don't mess around with dead ladies," he said, shaking his head. "As a matter of fact, I don't even mess around with live ones."

With a meaningful gesture he pushed his empty glass closer to the bottle, but Lowee was not about to let him shrug off the subject. Lowee touched his arm in a confidential gesture.

"Did you know they seen her around here a lot?"

DeKok lost all pretense.

"You mean, here . . . here in the neighborhood?"

Little Lowee nodded while he refilled DeKok's glass.

"She ain't never been in here, but I heard about her from some of the girls. And Old Bart, the music-man, he saw her in the alley, you know."

"When?" asked DeKok sharply.

"Oh, before the cops got there. He come in here white as a sheet and wants a beer. Then he told us what he had seen. The girls thought it was one of them and asked what she looked like. Bart told 'em. Good looking dame, blonde . . . weren't she?"

"Yes."

"Well, some of the girls knew who it were right-a-way."

"She was that well known?"

The barkeeper shrugged.

"You don't see many strange dames around here. It's mostly men, ain't it? I knows all the working girls and they knows each other. When they see a strange dame they always do worry about competition."

DeKok stared thoughtfully in his glass.

"Did she look like competition?"

Lowee shook his head.

"No, no, no . . . don't take it that way. You knows how they is. Every woman in the Quarter is looked over. There's too many of them heroine whores as it is. The girls don't like it. So, when a new woman shows up, the girls look 'er over."

"To see if she's competition?"

"Exactum! That's all. But none of the girls said nothing about her stealing customers."

"So, what was she doing around here?"

The little barkeeper raised his arms in the air.

"How should I know? I didn't even know her. Maybe she had a boy-friend in the neighborhood. Or maybe she met somebody here. It wouldn't be the first time."

DeKok sipped from his cognac while he assimilated the new information. He looked at Little Lowee from over the rim of his glass. Then he replaced the glass on the counter and raked his hand through his hair, almost absent mindedly lifting his hat to make the gesture possible.

"She was a beautiful woman," he said dully. "A very beautiful woman." He shook his head in sadness. "They strangled her, just like that." He paused, there seemed to be a

49

lump in his throat. "Just like that," he repeated. "Maybe she knew something or maybe some guy had had enough of her."

Little Lowee swallowed. The sentimentality, that is so much a part of the true Amsterdammer, was rising to the surface.

"What a rotten trick," he managed from the bottom of his heart.

DeKok nodded with emphasis.

"You're right Lowee . . . a rotten trick. That's why I would like to catch him, lock him up. You get me? I'd love to see how he'd like *that*." He paused for effect, but also to gather his thoughts. "Do me a favor, Lowee, find out what the girls know. They may know something important, maybe they saw where she went, whom she met."

Lowee picked up his glass and drained it in one long swallow.

"Count on me, DeKok," he said with determination in his voice. "As soon as I hear somewhat . . ."

The gray sleuth interrupted with a smile.

"Thanks, Lowee, on that note, just this once, pour me one for the road."

* * *

As if he did not have a care in the world, DeKok strolled through the narrow streets and along the ancient canals of his beloved Amsterdam. He looked at the well-known landmarks and familiar sights as if he was a tourist. He never wearied of the sights and sounds of the old city. Eventually he reached his destination and stepped into Aunt Mia's Coffeehouse. With a playful gesture he tickled the chin of the fat proprietress and walked through to the back of the public room. There, in a corner, he found Old Bart, the music-man, as he was known in the Quarter. In his younger days he played the accordion and accompanied himself on a mouth organ, while a pair of cymbals, tied to his knees, would beat the rhythm. These days, he just barely managed the accordion by itself. The old man stared at a pitifully small heap of dimes, quarters and pennies, the harvest of a long musical trip from one bar to the next. Idly he pushed the coins in rows, sorting them by denomination.

Annoyed, he looked up when the gray sleuth sank down on a chair across from him. A defensive, hostile look came over him.

"Did I ask for you?" he growled.

DeKok grimaced.

"I'm like death," he said in sepulcher tones, "I come unannounced."

Old Bart waved him away.

"I'd just as soon see you leave. I don't like cops. They stink."

DeKok snorted.

"Money doesn't stink," he said sharply.

A cunning look came in the old musician's eyes.

"What do you mean?"

"Exactly what I say . . . money doesn't stink. Even when it comes from the purse of a dead woman."

The old man stood up abruptly, he almost upset the table and some coins rolled away into the corners.

"You shut up," he yelled vehemently. "I hold no truck with your stories, your accusations, your . . . your *indecent* slander. I never touched her purse."

A look of utter disbelief settled on DeKok's face.

"You didn't?" he asked scornfully.

"No . . . stealing from the dead . . ." There was genuine indignation in the old man's voice. "You don't . . . you just don't, that's all, it's . . . it's obscene. *That's* what it is, obscene. You have the wrong guy, this time, DeKok." He slapped his chest. "You don't want *me*."

"Then, who *do* I want?"

Old Bart gesticulated.

"That guy!"

"What guy?"

"The guy that walked out of the alley."

DeKok placed a friendly hand on the musician's shoulder and pressed him back into his seat.

"Sit down," he cajoled. "Sit down and tell me exactly what happened."

Old Bart swallowed. DeKok's lightning attack had confused him, shocked him, upset him. With a crooked, arthritic hand he swiped the coins toward him. His lower lip trembled as he heaped them together.

"I . . . I'd been to Red Fred's bar," he began, stammering with delayed indignation. "I go there a lot, to Fred's, I mean. It's a good bar for me. Some guy at the bar had bought me a few beers, five, six maybe, and when I came outside I had to piss." He pointed at the accordion. "That isn't easy with a squeeze box in front of your stomach."

DeKok nodded understanding.

"So, you decided to take a piss in the alley."

"And why not? Everybody does it!"

DeKok soothed him.

"Yes, yes, I know. Then what happened?"

"Well, I stood, I think about halfway down the alley when I saw the guy, just where the alley makes a bend, you know? Well, I saw this guy and he was all bent over, you know what I mean, as if he was doing something to the pavement."

"Go on."

"I know it sounds crazy, but that's what I thought he was doing. After a few seconds he straightened out and looked in my

52

direction. When he saw me he seemed to hesitate and for just a moment I thought he was going to come after me. But then he suddenly turned and ran away."

"Toward St. John's Street?"

"Yes, that way. When I finished my business I went over to look. You see, I was just curious to find out what he had been doing to the pavement."

"And you found the woman."

Old Bart nodded.

"Yes, near the lamppost. She was in a peculiar position and I looked in her eyes. I saw at once that she was dead." He paused, as if reminiscing, then he added: "But I never touched her handbag!"

DeKok ignored the last remark.

"What sort of guy was it?"

The musician shrugged his shoulders.

"A guy . . . a tall guy . . . about mid thirties, I'd say, maybe a bit younger." He made an apologetic gesture. "There isn't a lot of light in the alley and I wasn't exactly in a position to take a good look, you know what I mean, not as if you could just look at everything at leisure."

DeKok looked searchingly at the old man for a long time, with a little finger he rubbed the bridge of his nose.

"You know, Bart," he said at length, "I don't believe there was a guy at all. You're only telling me this because I accused you of stealing money from her purse."

The old man became red in the face.

"I stole nothing," he shouted wildly. "I . . . do . . . NOT . . . rob . . . the . . . dead!"

DeKok rose and shook his head at the old man.

"I never believed it," he said, without clarifying what it was he did not believe. He fished a guilder from his pocket and placed it on the table.

"To replace the coins that rolled away."

6

Vledder looked at his mentor with a confused look on his face.

"But why not? Old Bart could easily have seen some guy in the alley."

DeKok started the slow ritual that, Vledder knew, would eventually result in him finding a piece of forgotten candy somewhere about his person.

"You're right," he admitted resignedly. "He saw somebody. I'm convinced of that."

"But you said . . ."

DeKok raised a protesting hand.

"Old Bart really hates cops. It goes back years and years, really. He used to get a lot of tickets in the old days, making music without a permit, disturbing the peace, playing music in the public roadway, you know how that goes, nuisances. Somebody complains and the police have to respond. But Old Bart always took it very personally, he bears us a permanent grudge. If I had asked him straight out if he had seen anything peculiar in the alley, he would have said nothing, or would have lied about it."

Vledder smiled.

"So you accused him of theft."

DeKok shook his head ruefully, as if ashamed of his actions.

"Yes, I could not count on his voluntary cooperation, I had to provoke him." He smiled wanly. "It was most unfair, Bart never stole anything in his life, never really committed any real crimes. In any case, he became angry and told me what I wanted to know. I'm sorry about it, really, I felt sorry for him, too."

Vledder mulled over DeKok's words. He and Bart had probably known each other while both were still young men. He wondered if DeKok, as a young constable, had ticketed the old musician. Then he realized that DeKok, even back then, would have found a way to get around that.

"But," said the young man after a while, "I still don't understand why you're so suddenly convinced that he really did see someone in the alley. I thought your theory about making up a fictitious character to keep himself blameless, quite reasonable."

DeKok, as Vledder knew he would, had found a piece of candy and popped it in his mouth. He sucked contently while he reflected on Vledder's words. Sometimes the boy speaks like a written report, he thought, he should watch that.

Aloud he said:

"There was that little twist in Bart's story that convinced me. He said that the man hesitated when he saw Bart. That convinced me. The killer, at least the person who was bent over the lifeless body of Juliette's body, asked himself momentarily how much danger there was from the witness, how damaging it could be. He had a choice . . ."

He stopped. Reflecting on his own words, he thought he was as bad as Vledder. We are all becoming machines, he scolded himself, mouthing platitudes and catch-phrases.

Vledder, unaware of DeKok's thoughts and with his penchant for repeating the obvious, looked at his partner.

"You mean," he said, "that for a moment he actually contemplated whether or not he should . . ."

DeKok nodded.

"That's why I told Old Bart I didn't believe it. I didn't want him to think that what he told me was important. I'd just as soon he forgets all about it and doesn't discuss it any further."

"And if he does?"

DeKok sighed.

"Let's hope the killer doesn't find out." He moved in his chair, then changed the subject. "What about the autopsy?" he asked.

Vledder shrugged his shoulders.

"Pretty unproductive. Not much new information. According to the pathologist, Juliette's death was the result of being throttled to death. A particularly powerful strangulation. The killer was definitely somebody with strong hands. Some of the cartilage, part of the windpipe, in the neck had been crushed."

DeKok pushed his lower lip forward.

"That's some force. But Dr. Rusteloos doesn't agree with Dr. Koning about the cause of death?"

"Strangulation?"

"No, no, I mean the marks on the side of her neck."

Vledder shook his head.

"This morning they were hardly visible, almost faded away. I *did* point it out to Dr. Rusteloos, but he did not consider it important."

"But strangulation, nevertheless?"

"Yes, without a doubt. Why the questions? The slight marks on the side of the neck, according to Dr. Rusteloos, could have been caused by clothing, he suggested the abrasive effect of a sharp, starched collar."

DeKok looked thoughtful.

"What about a necklace?" he asked.

"A necklace?"

Vledder's eyes lit up.

"Of course," he said, excitement in his voice, "of course. That's the answer. A necklace, brutally torn off, broken. Dr. Rusteloos was right, the marks in her neck are not important . . . at least, not in connection with the cause of death." He slapped his hand flat on the desk. "But they are important to us . . . as a clue about the killer." He cocked his head and looked at DeKok. "What about," he said slyly, "if you called that *maitre d'* back and asked him . . ."

DeKok smiled.

"This morning you were joking that I even knew what they had for dinner. Well, I knew a little more than that. I've also been told what they were wearing."

Vledder looked expectantly.

"A necklace?"

DeKok nodded, ending the suspense.

"An expensive necklace with a heavy pendant, an old-fashioned cameo, set in gold lace and decorated with red rubies. I wrote it down the way the man told me. He had noticed it especially, because it reminded him of some old aunt who had a similar medallion."

Vledder stared into the distance.

"She wasn't wearing it when we found her," he said thoughtfully.

"No, it was torn away and that caused the marks on her neck."

Vledder looked at his old friend. There was a frown on his young face.

"You knew already, this morning, before I left." There was reproach in his voice.

DeKok waved away his objections.

"I merely suspected it, that's all. I wasn't sure at all, at all. There was no way to be sure that the marks in her neck had nothing to do with her being strangled. If it had not been a necklace, it could have been caused by some other item used to kill her, a rope, a scarf. I had to wait for the autopsy." He smiled. "Dr. Koning isn't the only one who doesn't spread rumors *before* an autopsy," he added.

"Quite right," said Vledder, absent-mindedly, parroting his mentor. Then: "Who could have taken the medallion . . . the killer?"

DeKok pulled his lower lip forward and let it plop back. He repeated the annoying gesture several times.

"That's the most likely possibility," he said finally. "But who knows, the marks could have happened earlier, during sex, maybe, or during a quarrel. I think it's time you find out where we can reach 'friend' Bearburgh. It's about time we ask him a few pertinent questions."

* * *

Standing on the porch of his large house at the lake, casually dressed in shorts and a sweater, Andrew Bearburgh looked with surprise at the two Inspectors.

"What . . . W-what are you doing here?" he stuttered. "I mean, I didn't summon you."

DeKok made a helpless gesture.

"Today I'm definitely *persona non grata,*" he sighed. "This is the second time in one day that somebody isn't happy to see me."

Vledder pulled a pathetic face.

"You may find this hard to believe," the younger man added sadly, "but we, tired representatives of the Law, have a difficult life. We're simply not appreciated."

Andrew Bearburgh looked irate.

"Spare me your self-pity," he said angrily. "I'll ask you just one more time . . . what are you doing here?"

DeKok pointed past him, into the corridor of the house.

"Won't you ask us to come in?" he asked with sweet sarcasm. "Your hospitality is well-know."

"Yes," added Vledder, overdoing it, "people stop us in the street and remark upon your hospitality all the time."

Vledder was often annoyed with DeKok when the latter engaged in what Vledder called "cheap theatricals". Like many on the force, he always wondered that people never saw through DeKok's obvious mannerisms and dramatic gestures. They never did. But whenever Vledder tried to do the same, it usually wound up being either heavy-handed, or lost its effect altogether. It was an added source of frustration for the young policeman.

Bearburgh looked at the two for a while, seemed of two minds about his response.

"Come in," he said finally, ungraciously.

As the two men climbed the steps to the porch, he continued.

"I had not expected your visit. You have me at a disadvantage, so to speak. I'm busy with the preparations for the funeral and the last thing I expected was visitors. Invitations, you know." He smiled deprecatingly, apologetically. "A touchy subject, I can tell you."

DeKok's eyebrows rippled briefly. As usual, he was totally unaware of the action. Bearburgh looked startled, then he absorbed DeKok's remark.

"Have you been appointed?" asked DeKok. "I mean, did the family appoint you to make the arrangements?"

"Appointed?" snorted Bearburgh. "I haven't heard a thing from the precious Weers. Not so much as an expression of condolence, or anything. I take it that you have informed the family?"

DeKok nodded.

"We made sure that they were notified as soon as possible."

Andrew snorted again.

"The Weer family," he said derisively, "are a bunch of degenerates. Far be it from me to try and influence you, but you'll soon find out. Mark my words, they're completely amoral."

He led the Inspectors from a bare, white-tiled corridor to a sitting room. The room was wide, high and roomy, sparsely furnished with an ultra modern decor where chrome and black and white lacquer dominated. The room had large windows and was as appealing and cozy as the steel skeleton of a bank building.

DeKok shivered as he entered the room. The room was as cold, cool and businesslike as a slaughterhouse. Every semblance of homeyness seemed to have been consciously barred. The chill seemed to envelop the visitor. He thought about the house on the Mirrors Canal and with a sudden insight guessed why the marriage between this man and the victim had failed. Despite his heated tone and impulsive behavior, Andrew Bearburgh was capable of little warmth . . . little real love.

"Sit down." A slender, languid hand waved at a chrome skeleton with pillows against the wall. "How can I be of service?"

DeKok gave him his best smile.

"Our visit is no more than a formality," he began soothingly. "You could call it a courtesy call. Yes, a courtesy call, that's the way to look at it. We were just curious how you liked your dinner, last night?"

Andrew's face which had relaxed slightly when DeKok began to speak, became void of expression as he finished. He looked searchingly at the two Inspectors and did not answer at once.

"So, you know about that," he sighed finally, resignedly. "You're right, yes. Juliette and I had dinner together last night. I invited her to have dinner with me in the Amstel hotel." He paused and suddenly changed his tone. "Is that against the Law?" he asked in a loud tone of voice. "Why can't a man invite his ex-wife to dinner? Is that prohibited?"

DeKok sat down, leaned into the foam rubber.

"There's no law against having dinner." he said dryly.

Andrew Bearburgh gave him a dirty look.

"I didn't kill her," he said.

Vledder shook his head.

"We never said that . . . not yet. But you *are* a candidate."

"Candidate?"

Vledder nodded slowly.

"A candidate for arrest."

Bearburgh grinned sheepishly.

"You're joking."

But Vledder was not to be stopped. DeKok watched with an indulgent inner smile. His face was expressionless.

Vledder stretched an arm in the direction of Bearburgh, perfectly imitating the languid gesture with which their host had invited them to be seated.

"Let me explain," he said patiently. "Juliette was found in Slate Makers Alley at exactly twenty-seven minutes past midnight. No doubt you read that in the papers. According to the coroner and since confirmed by the pathologist, at that time she had been dead for at least three to six hours. You and she left the Amstel hotel shortly after eight o'clock. It's simple mathematics: you were the last person to see her alive."

Bearburgh took a step in the direction of the young detective. His manner was aggressive, threatening. His fists were balled.

"I didn't kill her," he hissed, close to Vledder's face.

Vledder shrugged his shoulders nonchalantly.

"You've said that before," he answered airily. "I'm not impressed. I have never yet met a murderer who confessed at once. Usually it takes a few days."

Andrew Bearburgh looked at DeKok with a beseeching look in his eyes.

"Why don't you say something?" he whined "And tell him to shut up."

DeKok made a powerless gesture.

"What do you expect? I cannot prevent my worthy colleague from revealing an obvious theory. The simple statement that you're not the killer satisfies no one. Me neither. You cannot deny that you were still seen in her company at eight o'clock that night and she was still alive at that time."

Bearburgh covered his face in despair. His face was gray.

"I don't want to deny anything," he cried out. "There's nothing to deny! I'm NOT her killer! I didn't do it!"

"Really?"

The question combined sarcasm and disbelief and seemed to take the last bit of energy from their host. He sank into a chair, exhausted.

"No," he whispered tiredly. "Believe me, I'm not your man. Juliette and I were not a harmonic pair. Far from it. I'd be the last to deny *that*. Our married life was, to put it mildly, stormy. Hundreds of times I may have felt like killing her. Even after the divorce there were plenty of occasions when I would have cheerfully wrung her beautiful neck. But I can only repeat what I've said before: I'm not your man. I'm not her killer. And . . . I'm not the last person to have seen her alive."

Vledder looked at him with astonishment.

"What?"

Andrew shook his head.

"No, the last man to see her alive was Jonathan."

"Who's Jonathan?"

"Her brother. She had a date with him."

7

DeKok lifted both legs on top of his desk and leaned comfortably back in his chair. He was not at all disappointed. The case seemed to progress satisfactorily, he was making headway.

Vledder pushed his chair closer so that it would be easier to talk over the constant hub-bub in the large detective room. At times the noise could be deafening.

"Friend Bearburgh," he smirked, "had little resistance to offer, don't you agree? He broke rather quickly. What do you think of his story?"

DeKok pursed his lips.

"Why don't we go over it. It seems important enough."

Vledder took out his ubiquitous little note book and flipped through the pages.

"Andrew Bearburgh," he began, "stated that he drove his ex-wife, at her request, straight from the Amstel Hotel to Dam Square. Juliette was in a hurry because, according to Andrew, she had an appointment with her brother Jonathan and she didn't want to keep him waiting. Andrew, showing off, ignores a number of stoplights and the posted speed limits, but is unable to get her there on time. It's about seven minutes past eight when he drops her off in front of Hotel Krasnapolsky. His last view of her is the image in his rear view mirror as she waved after him.

Andrew returns happily directly to his house on the lake in order to change. During dinner Juliette had promised to spend the night with him and, to give substance to his hopes, she had given him a key to her house on the Mirrors Canal."

Vledder looked up from his notes.

"Is that normal, when you're divorced?"

DeKok scratched the back of his neck, mulling over Vledder's words. It was always a marvel to him how, based on the cryptic notes he scribbled down, the young man could come up with phrases that seemed a cross between an official report and a romantic novel. Then, realizing Vledder had asked a question, he answered:

"Don't ask me. I've no experience with that. I've been married to the same woman for more than twenty five years." He grinned to himself. "But, regardless, Andrew's story seems reasonable. It agrees with the facts as we know them and it can easily be checked."

"You mean, we'll check with the hotel?"

"Definitely. I'm sure they know our Juliette very well. Also, you'll have the enlargement from the passport photo. Just check and ask the personnel who were on duty at the time. You know," he added thoughtfully, "Hotel Krasnapolsky is barely a hundred yards from Slate Makers Alley." He paused. "As the crow flies," he amplified.

Vledder looked interested.

"Surely you don't think she was killed in Krasnapolsky?"

Slowly DeKok shook his head.

"No, too risky. The killer would have had to reserve a room. We can check the register, of course, but I don't believe it. Registering in a hotel would create all sorts of complications for the killer. And then," he added as if the thought just occurred to him, "how are you going to get a dead woman out of the hotel without being seen?"

He lifted his legs from the desk and leaned closer to Vledder.

"But we're close, real close."

Vledder smiled.

"Closer than the crow flies?"

DeKok shook his head patiently.

"No, not place . . . but time." His tone was indulgent. "I mean that little arithmetic problem you presented to Andrew, earlier. There's very little time between seven minutes past eight and the time of death."

Vledder pressed his lips together. He looked determined.

"Somebody," he said, "has a lot of explaining to do."

DeKok nodded agreement.

"Brother Jonathan," he said.

There was a long pause. Both men were occupied with their own thoughts, the noise in the room seemed to recede, as if they were wrapped in private cocoons.

Suddenly the cone of companionable silence was pierced.

"So, this is where you're hiding," exclaimed Inspector Bonmeyer.

DeKok looked at him in surprise.

"Where else?"

Bonmeyer looked wronged.

"I've been all over the building, less than fifteen minutes ago, and you were nowhere to be found." He sounded victimized. "I know better than to try to get you on the radio," he added.

DeKok's eyebrows did a little dance, sufficient to distract Bonmeyer for a few seconds.

"We just got back a little while ago," clarified DeKok. "You must have missed us. What's the matter?"

Bonmeyer gestured with his head.

"The Commissaris needs you."

"Again?"

"Yes, he has visitors ... old Mrs. Weer and her son, Jerome."

* * *

"DeKok ... with kay-oh-kay."

Old Mrs. Weer rose from her chair and stretched out a wrinkled hand.

"You're the man," she said evenly, "who will find the murderer of my daughter."

DeKok glanced at the Commissaris

"That sounds as if somebody made you a promise," he said gently. "But I may have to disappoint you. I can't promise anything at this stage, but you have my word that I will do everything in my power to make the promise come true."

Mrs. Weer gave him a wan smile.

"Your name is my guarantee. I've heard a lot about you and I know that you will serve truth and justice."

DeKok looked at her with a long, penetrating look.

"Truth," he answered seriously, "is often an uncomfortable master and justice ... justice is open to many interpretations."

The old lady leaned forward, acknowledging his statement with old-world grace.

"I understand," she said softly.

DeKok turned toward Jerome and shook hands with him.

"I see the family is not all here."

Jerome did not answer at once, but looked at his mother.

"Brother Jonathan," he hesitated, "was ... eh, was unable to come."

Mrs. Weer reacted sharply. Her small brown eyes flashed behind the thick lenses of her glasses.

"Tell it like it is, Jerome," she scolded. "There's no use telling lies to the police." She turned toward DeKok. "The truth is," she explained, "that we have no idea about Jonathan's whereabouts. He has disappeared."

DeKok managed to hide his surprise behind an expressionless face.

"Since when?"

She pursed her lips into a circle of fine wrinkles.

"Since about a week ago, isn't it, Jerome? We have heard nothing and seen hide nor hair of him for some time. He's probably on the Riviera."

Jerome nodded agreement.

"Yes," he said, "in the South of France. When his money runs out, he'll be back."

Mrs. Weer smiled tenderly.

"Jonathan has always been a strange child," she explained. "A bit of a worry. We've had to clean up a number of his affairs, over the years, isn't that so, Jerome? Usually without my husband knowing about it."

"What sort of affairs?"

The old lady waved as if the subject had lost all importance.

"Gambling debts, women. You know how it is. Girls who claim to be pregnant, blackmail games by disreputable characters, insulted husbands. I've seen them all come and go. Jonathan just lives it up and he's always short of cash." As shadow fell over her face. "Juliette had a similar character. In a way I'm not surprised."

DeKok gave her another long, penetrating look.

"You mean her . . . her sudden death?"

She sighed deeply.

"It's my husband's fault. He was never able to refuse her anything. She was the apple of his eyes, his favorite. He indulged her in everything." She shook her head. "That is never right. I

69

often told Henry that he was creating weak characters. Juliette is a case in point. She never knew the proprieties. She had no sense of *proportion*." She bit her lower lip. Suddenly she lost her poise and her eyes filled with tears. Nervously she reached for her handbag and took out a handkerchief. "Juliette," she whispered, ". . . my child, my poor child." She looked up at DeKok. "How can anybody *do* such a thing?"

DeKok did not answer. He avoided the old woman's eyes and looked outside. He had asked the same question so often during his long career. Why would anybody kill his fellow man? Revenge, greed, envy?

Commissaris Buitendam intervened smoothly.

"The reasons," he said formally, "can be many." He made a deferential, apologetic gesture. "We would be a lot closer to the solution if we knew the motive."

Mrs. Weer took both of DeKok's hands in her own.

"You *will* find him, won't you, Mr. DeKok? You will find him!"

There was such a plaintive tone to her voice that DeKok, despite himself, felt a lump in his throat.

"I'll find him," he answered softly, but firmly.

Jerome stood up.

"Let's go, Mother. We still have to go see Andrew."

The old lady rose carefully. She was again in control of herself. The tears had been dried and the momentary weakness had passed. DeKok watched the transformation but kept his own counsel.

"Will you come visit me tonight?" she asked. "Eight o'clock? Would that be convenient? You know where I live?"

DeKok nodded.

"Yes, South Walk Way."

"Exactly, number 235. Not far from the Amstel, the river, not the hotel. Will you bring Inspector Vledder?"

"If you wish."

"Very much. You two have worked together for a long time, haven't you?"

"Many years."

Mrs. Weer smiled.

"I have an excellent cognac at home. I've been told you're a connoisseur." She hesitated, changed her tone of voice, then added: "I may be able to tell you something that might be pertinent to your investigation."

"Why not tell me now?"

"No, no, later, I must be sure."

DeKok bowed with old-world charm.

"We'll look forward to it," he said sincerely.

The old lady took her leave from the Commissaris. Jerome, too, shook his hand. DeKok watched from a distance, cool, sharply observant without so much as the flicker of an eyelid. Just before mother and son were to leave the room, he stepped forward.

"If you hear anything about Jonathan. . .," he paused, ". . . please let me know. I'm interested in his whereabouts. I do, you see, have reasons to believe that he had an appointment with Juliette, shortly before her death."

Jerome swallowed.

"Shortly before her death?" he repeated.

"Indeed."

"But . . . then . . . Jonathan." He did not complete the sentence, but looked at his mother. The warning glance in her eyes did not escape DeKok's observation.

The old woman smiled graciously.

"If we hear anything at all about Jonathan," she said in a friendly tone of voice, "we'll most certainly let you know. Isn't that so, Jerome?"

Jerome looked pale.

71

* * *

"How did it go? How was the old man?"

DeKok grinned.

"As nice as could be, this once. But then, he had little choice."

"How's that?"

"He had made a solemn promise to Mrs. Weer and her son that I would find Juliette's murderer in no time at all, at all."

Vledder looked at him from aside, a smile on his lips.

"A sign of confidence, he trusts you."

DeKok shook his head.

"I could have done without that promise. First, it remains to be seen if I can live up to it and second . . . I wonder if Mrs. Weer really wants me to find the killer."

"What!?"

"Yes, I'm not sure she wants the killer found."

Vledder looked astonished.

"Why-ever not?"

DeKok rose from his chair and went over to the window. Balancing on the balls of his feet he looked down into Warmoes Street and watched Moshe, the herring man, maneuver his cart into the narrow Corner Alley.

"She gripped my hands," he said slowly, reliving the moment, "and begged me to find Juliette's killer. Very, very dramatic, very theatrical. It seemed genuine. Perhaps it was, as long as . . ."

"As long as the killer isn't Jonathan."

DeKok nodded. The sight of Moshe made his mouth water with the thought of fresh, raw herring, liberally covered with raw onions.

"Exactly," he said. "If it turns out that Jonathan is the guilty party, we can expect little help from the Weer family. They even

72

tried to make me believe that Jonathan had been in the South of France for some time."

Vledder came to stand next to him.

"Did you tell them about the date between Juliette and Jonathan?"

DeKok resolutely turned his thoughts away from herring. "Not right away. I waited until they were just about to leave. The result was most satisfying."

Vledder grinned maliciously.

"I know that about you, an old trick. A friendly *coupe de grace* in closing, when they least expect it." He paused and looked at Moshe. It was his turn to think about the indescribable, heavenly taste of raw herring. Then, just as resolutely as DeKok, he concentrated on the matter at hand. "So," he continued, "before you had told them about Jonathan's date with Juliette, they tried to convince you he was in the South of France?"

"Yes."

Vledder, gripped by sudden inspiration, lost all caution. His natural exuberance and enthusiasm took over. His eyes sparkled.

"But, DeKok," he said excitedly, "that means that they considered it, counted on it and tried to account *for* it."

"What *are* you talking about?"

"They considered the possibility that Jonathan could be the killer and they tried to provide him with an alibi."

DeKok stared at nothing in particular.

"Could be," he said after a while. "Could be. Certainly an alibi that would be hard to break. The Riviera is so long and has so many hidden corners, out-of-the-way places, he could have been anywhere." He glanced at Vledder. "A shrewd observation," he added.

The younger man accepted the praise silently.

"What about an APB? For questioning?"

"For Jonathan . . . as a murder suspect?"

"Yes, of course."

DeKok shook his head.

"No, the case is still too weak for such a drastic measure. I mean, what do we have? All we really have to go on, is Andrew Bearburgh's declaration that Juliette had a date with her brother."

Vledder smiled ruefully.

"Yes, well, if you put it that way, it isn't much."

"Exactly. We will need a lot more before we can ask for his apprehension. At this moment Jonathan is no more than a possible witness." He raked his fingers through his hair. "But," he went on, "you *can* put the medallion on the telex. Perhaps it'll surface somewhere."

Vledder turned around, opened a drawer and took out a message form. Quickly he started to fill in the required information. Suddenly he stopped and looked at DeKok.

"I have a surprise for you. I almost forgot."

DeKok gave him a suspicious look.

"A nice surprise?"

The young Inspector waved impatiently.

"While you were busy with the Commissaris and the Weers, I went to Krasnapolsky."

"So?"

"Juliette was never there."

"Was not there?" DeKok sounded puzzled.

Vledder shook his head.

"That's right, she was not there during the night of the murder."

"What about brother Jonathan?"

Vledder sighed elaborately.

"The estimates vary considerably, but it's certain that brother Jonathan hasn't been near the Hotel Krasnapolsky for weeks."

"Both were well known?"

"Oh, yes. Very well known. I didn't even need the photograph. The doorman, the lobby personnel, the waiters, they all knew immediately who I was talking about. Jonathan, too, used to be a regular visitor until recently. He used to spend a lot of time in the bar. Brother and sister were seldom, however, seen together." Vledder looked at DeKok. "What do you think?" he asked. "Do you think Andrew deliberately misled us?"

DeKok shook his head slowly, thoughtfully.

"I don't think so, at least, that's not the impression I got. Don't forget, Juliette *never* said she had an appointment *in* the Hotel. She only asked Andrew to drop her off *at* the Krasnapolsky."

"You mean, that the Krasnapolsky didn't necessarily have to be the meeting place?" asked Vledder, again demonstrating his ability to ask superfluous questions. DeKok knew, however, that it was the young man's way to place information firmly in his mind. Therefore he answered patiently.

"That's right. Of course, it was the most obvious conclusion that they were to meet *there*, but they could have arranged anywhere else, just as easily."

DeKok walked over to the large map of Amsterdam's inner city which was prominently displayed on the wall and which showed in a thick, red outline the boundaries of the Warmoes Street district.

"Wherever they agreed to meet, it wasn't far from where she got out of the car. The appointment was for eight o'clock and she was in a hurry. She was late already." Pensively he tapped the map with an index finger. "Believe me," he continued, "she would never have gotten out of the car at that point if she could have been driven closer to the appointed place."

"I can understand that," remarked Vledder, "some places around there are almost impassable for a bicycle, let alone a car. She must have known about a short-cut."

DeKok, who was well-known for his opinion that the best way to get around the city was on foot, did not bother to comment immediately.

"Yes," he said finally, tapping the map again. "Yes, I *do* believe in that appointment. As far as that was concerned, Juliette had nothing to hide from Andrew. There was nothing suspicious about a date with Jonathan, with her brother. She could openly talk about that even with jealous Andrew. You see," he explained, "for a while I toyed with the idea that Juliette had just made up an appointment with Jonathan, in order to hide the fact that she was meeting another man. But I had to let that thought go. That night, no matter how frivolous she might have been, Juliette was not involved in any adventures."

"But why not?"

"There was no time, no need."

Vledder smiled knowingly.

"Of course, she had already promised the night to her ex-husband."

DeKok laughed.

"Excellent, really excellent." He raised a forefinger in an admonishing way. "Mind you," he said didactically, "despite her appointment with Jonathan, she had promised Andrew to spend the night with him. Also, she had accepted Andrew's invitation to dinner. We can assume," he added with a twinkle in his eye, "that Juliette knew her ex-husband well enough to know what that could lead to."

Vledder laughed out loud.

"Of course she knew," he explained. "She knew it so well that she had taken the precaution of carrying a second house key with her." He fell silent, plucked his lower lip in a subconscious imitation of a similar habit by DeKok. "But," he added, "that still leaves the puzzle of the eight o'clock appointment."

DeKok moved his hand aimlessly over the map.

"If Juliette Weer had to go to Krasnapolsky to keep her appointment with death," he asked, "what was her ultimate destination?"

Vledder grimaced.

"Slate Makers Alley," he said bitterly. It was meant as a frivolous answer, but it fell flat. DeKok reacted strangely, almost confused.

"Slate Makers Alley," he repeated dreamily. "We haven't yet looked there in the full light of day."

8

They strolled through the Quarter, DeKok half a step ahead, nonchalant, untidy, with his hands buried deep in the pockets of his trousers and his decrepit little felt hat far back on his head. Vledder was neater, less *bon-vivant*, in a conservative suit, blond short hair and well groomed.

They turned right toward Front Fort Canal as they progressed in silence. DeKok stopped briefly on Old Church Square and passed the time of day with Red Tina, one of the many whores he had known for a lifetime. Vledder came closer. He listened as DeKok asked with genuine interest after the welfare of a host of relatives. The young Inspector was not the least bit interested. A bit bored, impatient, he waited until DeKok would terminate the conversation. Suddenly he sharpened his ears.

"Too bad, wasn't it, about that girl in Slate Makers Alley. She must have been a nice girl, or so I heard. I talked to her mother, the old lady was heartbroken."

Red Tina cocked her head and looked at him. The lively face became serious.

"It's a sin," she said sadly. "They just kill anything that moves. You know, Mr. DeKok, it's all the fault of the psychiatrists. They just mess around. Everything is permitted nowadays."

DeKok ignored the change of subject.

"Some of you girls must have known her," he suggested.

Red Tina nodded with conviction.

"Oh, yes, we knew her." There was pity in her voice. "She often came by here."

"Alone?"

"Sometimes. But usually she was with a dark-haired guy. Slender, good looking chap. About thirty, I'd say. He was also dressed like he belonged to the country club. You know what I mean, turtle neck sweater, jacket with embroidery on the pocket, suede shoes. Like I said, a gentleman, but a bit of a softy."

DeKok smiled. No doubt Tina's assessment was correct. Nobody could judge a man better than a prostitute.

"You ever see her go in, anywhere around here?"

She shook her head.

"No, Lowee asked me the same question. No, I've never seen that. As I said, I just saw her pass by a few times. She used to come from the direction of High Street and she and her man would pass by the Old Church in the direction of Warmoes Street."

"Always the same man?"

She adjusted something. One hand went down the front of her blouse and moved from left to right. Then she closed a button.

"Ach," she said comfortably, "I didn't watch all that close, you know. If I happened to see her, I would say to myself: There's that good looking blonde again. That's all, you see. She wasn't in the life."

"Are you sure?"

Tina gave him a pitying smile.

"Are you sure?" she repeated. "Of course I'm sure, you can see that at once. No, she wasn't in the life. She was also . . . a real lady . . . a lady with standing. You know what I mean? Class . . . that's what she was, class." She tapped her ample bosom. "I don't mind telling you, whenever I saw her pass by, I looked at her with envy."

"Why?"

"She was young, good looking, had class and she was with this terrific guy."

"She's dead," said DeKok soberly.

The woman nodded.

"Yes, that's what I mean. You shouldn't envy anybody for what they have . . . for what they are." She stared dreamily into the distance. "Would you believe it, I actually would have liked to change places with her."

DeKok patted her shoulder in a fatherly gesture.

"I agree," he said. "You only know people from the outside . . . the shiny side that they show the world. One can look *at* it, but never *in* it." He gave her a sad smile. "Anyway, if you happen to hear something . . ."

He waved and walked away, followed by Vledder.

"What could Juliette have been doing in the neighbor-hood?"

DeKok shrugged his shoulders.

"I've asked myself the same question over and over. It seems as if she had a hideaway, a *pied-a-terre* somewhere around here. Perhaps a place to receive her friends, without being bothered by nosy neighbors, or unexpected visitors, some sort of love-nest."

Vledder glanced at him.

"And you think that's where she had the appointment with Jonathan?"

DeKok thought that over.

"Possibly," he said after a pause. "It would explain a lot, but . . . how do we find out?"

Vledder gestured around.

"Simple, we do a house-to-house search."

DeKok shook his head.

"That will take days, weeks and it *still* remains a guess whether or not you'll find it. Just look around you, from here you can see the Wester Tower. You forget that for years Anne Frank was hidden within sight of the Wester Tower, on the Prince's Canal. Hundreds of people, nobody will every know how many, were hidden away like that. Those hiding places still exist." He stopped, chewed his lower lip and then turned toward Vledder. "I've a better idea, I think. Why don't you go back to the station?"

"Why, what then?"

"Give your friend at the American Embassy a call and ask for a description of Mr. Summerfield. Find out if he's slender and dark-haired."

"And if he isn't?"

"Then you contact Andrew Bearburgh."

"Andrew?"

DeKok nodded emphatically.

"Yes, I presume he won't know about Juliette's . . . eh, love-nest in the Red Light District . . . But he will probably know about a good looking man, around thirty, as described by Tina." He smiled broadly. "Somehow, Andrew strikes me as the sort of man who knows all about the lovers of his ex-wife."

Vledder nodded easily.

"You're looking for the friend," he concluded.

"Indeed," agreed DeKok. "Let's hope he hasn't joined his Greek beauty in Athens. Then we're just as far as we were."

Vledder shook his head.

"I don't think it's Summerfield. Americans are not usually described as softies." Noticing the look in DeKok's eyes, he added hastily: "But I will check. Where can I find you?"

DeKok pushed his hat back a little further. It was now in danger of falling on the ground behind him.

"I'm going to take a long, leisurely look in Slate Makers Alley. Maybe I'll find something that we overlooked, last night."

Vledder snorted.

"And after that, it'll be Little Lowee's, I bet."

DeKok laughed heartily.

"Not a bad idea. When I'm at a total loss . . . Little Lowee has inspiration by the crate." He stretched out an arm, looked at his watch. "A nice cognac at this time of day . . . just one . . ." He did not finish the sentence but gave Vledder a worried look. "Will you remember to be back by eight?"

"Eight o'clock, tonight?"

DeKok nodded.

"I almost forgot. At eight o'clock we have an appointment at South Walk Way. You and me both. I was not to come alone. Old Mrs. Weer insisted that you should come along."

"Such an honor. To what do I owe that?"

DeKok looked serious.

"You owe it to assurance."

Vledder looked at him in surprise.

"Assurance?"

"Yes, assurance. She wants to make sure her words will not be lost, forgotten. She wants to make sure we *both* hear what she has to say. I'm convinced that she may have something important to say."

* * *

DeKok stood in the middle of Slate Makers Alley, his chin resting in his hand and a thoughtful look on his face. He tried to imagine how it would have looked some seventeen, eighteen hours ago when the killer placed his victim in the alley. It was dark then, of course, and the only light came from the single lamp post. He thought about the way the murderer had transported the dead woman. The alley was too narrow for a car, so he must have carried her, most probably in a fireman's grip.

But from what direction had he come? From the direction of St. John's Street, or Front Fort Canal? It was difficult to park a car at either end of the alley. But it was possible, there was no doubt about that. At least for a short time. And the killer had only needed seconds.

Old Bart, he thought, came from Red Fred's bar with his accordion draped across his stomach. Therefore the old music man must have come from the direction of Front Fort Canal into the alley *to perform outside privies and public rest rooms an act for which those accommodations are designated.** The man he had seen leaning over the corpse left the alley toward the other side, i.e., St. John's Street. Old Bart had the impression that the man first planned to come in *his* direction, but then changed his mind.

DeKok pulled his lower lip forward and let it plop back. Fortunately there was no one around to be annoyed by his least attractive habit. Could the car have been parked along Front Fort Canal and did the old man constitute an obstacle between the killer and his objective? Perhaps there was no car at all? But that would only complicate matters unnecessarily. Both Front Fort Canal and St. John's Street were relatively busy thoroughfares, even late at night. Definitely too busy to wander around with a

---

* Actual wording of the relevant Police Ordinance for Amsterdam.

corpse on one's shoulder without eliciting *some* sort of remark. Somebody would have seen him.

DeKok wiped the sweat from his forehead with the back of his sleeve. It was warm in the alley and it stank. The walls of the narrow alley seemed to breathe the penetrating smell of urine.

He walked up and down a few times and looked at the spot where the young woman had been found. There was nothing to be seen. Nothing that would help him create some order in his chaotic thoughts. In frustration he kicked the old lamp post. The dirty, narrow, stinking alley began to suffocate him. The atmosphere affected his mood, gnawed at his good humor, spoiled his equanimity. He longed for a large snifter of excellent cognac in the cool, semi-darkness of Little Lowee's bar. Hesitating, reluctantly he left the alley.

Suddenly he stopped in the middle of Front Fort Canal. He glanced at the water, looked at the houses, surveyed the narrow quay. A truck honked its horn at him and made him move hastily to the side. The driver rolled down his window, risking the heat into his air-conditioned cubicle, and cursed him soundly. The curses did not touch DeKok. Suddenly he saw again the scene surrounding the dead woman. In his mind's eye he went over the details. Juliette Weer, dressed in a chinchilla fur . . . on a balmy summer's evening. He grinned foolishly at himself. How stupid not to have noticed that before.

* * *

Young Vledder manoeuvred the old, sputtering police VW through Amsterdam's inner city. At a stoplight he glanced at DeKok who, as usual, was sprawled far down in his seat.

"It's an affront," complained Vledder.

DeKok looked at him as if aroused from a deep sleep.

"What?"

Vledder banged the dashboard with an angry fist.

"This heap of rust, this . . . this collection of scrap iron," he exclaimed angrily. "It's an insult to the city, to the police and . . . to us. We shouldn't have to appear in this wreck in the expensive driveway of 'Jolanda'."

"*Jolanda?*"

"Yes, that's the name of the Weer estate. I looked it up."

"I see. And you don't think you can make your appearance in a VW?"

"Right, it's an embarrassment."

DeKok slid back in his seat.

"I'll ask the Chief Commissaris if we may use a Rolls Royce, next time."

There was no denying the mockery in his voice. Cars, being modern, did not have DeKok's sympathy, or interest. To him it was just transportation. A form of transportation that by preference he used as little as possible.

Vledder looked pained. When the light turned to green, he savagely rammed the gearshift into second gear and pulled away, ignoring the whining protests of the underpowered engine.

* * *

DeKok understood full well what bothered his young colleague, partner and friend. The Amsterdam Municipal police drove around in old cars, was housed in old buildings with old furniture and locked suspects in old cells that had long been declared inadequate. DeKok would still get upset about the cells. The rest he accepted, had long since reconciled himself to the conditions. It had always been thus and *would* always be thus.

"Was it Summerfield?"

Vledder shook his head.

"Our man in Athens is tall, broad-shouldered and blond. He was raised in Texas on baked potatoes and chicken-fried steak."

DeKok laughed at the description.

"And what did Andrew have to say for himself?"

"Not much. He had a lot of trouble with the questions. At first he didn't even know who I was talking about. It was almost comical. Then he acted surprised. He began swearing. 'Well, dammit,' he said, 'it could be Jan, he's such a slimer.' and more words to that effect." Vledder smiled at the memory. "Naturally I asked him who Jan might be."

"Of course."

"It took a while before Andrew could get over his anger and surprise, but finally it came out. Jan ... Johannes Marie Antoine Drunnen in full, was a protege and confidant of old Henry Weer. Because of Henry he has an important job with CIH."

DeKok suddenly pulled himself into an upright position.

"Protege?" he asked. He pronounced the word as if it was something obscene.

Vledder nodded.

"Yes, he was almost a friend of the family. He was also aboard *Julia* when Henry died."

DeKok pushed his lower lip forward.

"Have you sent him an invitation?"

Vledder steered the car to the side of the road, braked and killed the engine.

"No," he sighed, "not yet. I couldn't get hold of him. I'll try again tonight, he may be home by then. He lives on Emperor Charles Way in the suburbs." He removed the key from the ignition and put it in his pocket. "This is as far as I go," he declared. "We walk the rest."

DeKok feigned horror.

"But it's another half mile, at least."

Vledder nodded, a determined look on his face.

"I know," he admitted, "but I'm not moving another inch in this rust bucket."

DeKok scratched the back of his neck and remained seated but eventually, with a deep sigh, he climbed out of the car. He looked at Vledder who waited for him next to the car. Slowly he raised his chin.

"Tell me," said DeKok with a playful smile around his lips, "is my tie straight?"

* * *

Jolanda, the Weer family estate was almost invisible from the street. It was hidden behind a curtain of green. The two Inspectors entered the driveway which was bordered by a hedge of pale pink roses and tall, slender birches. The gravel crunched under their feet. They stopped in front of the main entrance and then climbed the five steps to the wide patio. DeKok rang the bell and waited patiently. But nothing happened, no one came to open the door and no sound could be heard inside the building. DeKok looked at his watch. It was almost five minutes past eight. He rang the bell again, longer, more persistently.

Seconds, minutes went by and DeKok became impatient, restless. He felt the heavy oak door, decorated with intricate cast-iron ornaments. It was locked, impenetrable. With Vledder in his wake he moved around the building. Side entrances and back door were also closed and locked.

The gray sleuth felt in an inside pocket. His hand emerged with Handy Henkie's gift to him. It was a narrow copper tube that hid a number of ingenious picks, probes and other, less familiar instruments designed by the ex-burglar. Again Henkie's gift performed as before. The back door clicked open after just a few seconds. They moved quickly through the house, searched a labyrinth of corridors and rooms. But they found nobody.

Momentarily at a loss, DeKok looked around the large foyer. He was gripped by a strange, excited feeling. A premonition of something wrong, of something that had already happened.

Suddenly he stormed up the stairs to the second floor. Twice he opened the wrong door. Then he found old Mrs. Weer. She was in bed, fully dressed. Her hair formed a gray halo around her head.

DeKok stopped in the door opening as if suddenly paralyzed. Then his fists balled into angry lumps of flesh and a determined, hard look came into his eyes. Part of his mind felt Vledder's panting breath in his neck.

"Dead?"

DeKok nodded slowly, as if awakening from a trance.

"Murdered," he said.

9

DeKok placed the back of his hand against the cheek of the dead woman.

"She's cold," he said hoarsely. "It must have happened hours ago."

"Strangled?"

"I fear so."

Vledder leaned over the corpse.

"There's little to see on her neck."

DeKok took a deep breath.

"Not necessary," he said. "She's an old woman, thin and tawny." He looked at the wrinkled face, the dead, staring eyes and the slack, half-open mouth and shook his head. "She'll never say anything again," he concluded sadly.

Vledder nodded absent-mindedly.

"You think that's why . . .?"

DeKok did not answer. He walked away from the bed and proceeded to search the room. It was a large bedroom with a high ceiling, an alcove and an old-fashioned make-up table between two windows that looked out over a large, well-kept garden behind the house.

DeKok stood in front of one of the windows and looked outside. Everything was quiet and there was no movement. The setting sun threw long shadows from a privet hedge, a number of slender cypresses stood motionless in the windless night. It was a frozen setting, as if the garden mourned the passing of the old woman. He turned around and sniffed. The scent of lavender permeated everything, hung heavily in the air, dripped from the damask curtains. Lavender and old lace, thought Dekok, who could be easily moved at times like this.

"It's all so . . . peaceful," hesitated Vledder, also affected by the atmosphere in the room. "Almost natural. There's no sign of a struggle, or resistance. She must have submitted calmly to the killer."

DeKok looked past him. The words were heard, but did not register. The old lady's death had hit him unexpectedly, had surprised him. It was the last thing he had expected, especially this close after Juliette's death. He recalled his feeling that more murders were to follow, but old Mrs. Weer had not figured as one of the victims. It gave him an uncomfortable, guilty feeling, as if he had overlooked something.

"How can you prevent a murder?" he asked aloud.

Vledder looked at him, his intelligent face a study in surprise.

"Prevent?" he asked. "That's almost impossible to do. We can hardly guard every man, woman and child."

DeKok pressed his lips together. He had meant something entirely different, but he did not express it. Restlessly he paced up and down the room. He felt a compelling urge to release his tortured thoughts in a long series of eloquent curses, but the presence of the dead woman restrained him.

"Where's the staff?" he asked, irritated. "A house this size, with a garden to match . . . there should be servants."

Vledder shrugged his shoulders.

"I don't think there's anyone else in the house. You've seen for yourself, all doors were locked and nobody answered the bell."

DeKok nodded introspectively.

"They were locked, securely locked." It was as if he was repeating himself, tried to convince himself. Slowly he turned toward Vledder and gestured toward the lower floor.

"Downstairs, in the hall, there's a phone on a table. Call the coroner, the technical people, you know, the *Herd*. Then look around the house and see if you can find any obvious signs of breaking and entering . . . oh, yes, make sure they have the wherewithal to make plaster casts."

"Breaking and entering . . . plaster casts?"

DeKok waved impatiently.

"The perpetrator," he said, irked with Vledder's apparent slow comprehension, "must have come into the house somehow . . . and left somehow."

Vledder thought he understood.

"And if he had a key?"

Inspector DeKok looked for a long moment at his young friend, a penetrating, meaningful look.

"You will find," he said slowly, with emphasis, "that there *are* signs of breaking and entering . . . a busted door, an open skylight . . . a broken window. Believe me, you'll find it."

Vledder decided to drop the subject.

"All right," he said. "I'll call, I'll look. Anything else you want me to do?"

DeKok raked his fingers through his gray hair.

"Brother Jerome lives in Abcoude, that's only about seven miles from here. I'm sure his number will be somewhere near the phone. Ask him to come here at once."

"Shall I tell him . . .?"

DeKok shook his head.

"If he asks for particulars, just tell him that you have no time for explanations. But make sure he gets here, understand?"

Vledder nodded and left the room with a hesitant, wondering look in his eyes as he looked back over his shoulder. His old mentor could be strange, almost mystical, at times. Suddenly he could turn into an enigmatic person, impossible to follow, to understand. He could go off on a tangent that seemed to make no sense. It did not make it any more understandable, or palatable, that experience had shown that DeKok's apparent capricious behavior always had a purpose, always fitted into the pattern somewhere, somehow.

Thoughtfully he descended the staircase toward the hall. It was getting dark and the sparse light from the stained windows on either side of the door did little to dispel the gloom. The parquet floor squeaked under his feet.

After a number of phone calls he systematically searched the house. He went through all the rooms on the ground floor, the sitting room, the living room, the study, the smoking room with antique cuspidors in the corners, the game room dominated by an enormous billiard table, the kitchen large enough for a hotel, the pantry, the large dining room and a smaller dining room. Sharply observant his gaze traveled over furniture, along walls, floors and ceilings. At first glance there seemed to be nothing out of the ordinary, except for the richness and opulence of the surroundings. The scent of lavender was everywhere, even in the kitchen.

In one of the wings of the house he discovered a small office and an old fashioned *escritoire* against the wall. The desk was not locked and some papers were spread untidily across the green felt. A few drawers had been removed and were on the floor. Somebody had conducted a hasty search.

Suddenly he noticed that a pane of glass was missing from one of the windows. It was almost unnoticeable and when he came closer he saw that almost all the glass had been removed from the frame. A few splinters were all that remained. The opening was roughly twenty by thirty inches, almost two by three feet, he thought. Large enough to afford an easy passage to most people. Carefully, without touching anything, Vledder stuck his head through the window. In the waning light he could discern some glass splinters on the gravel below.

He went back to the hall.

"You're right," he called up the stairs, "there are signs of a break-in."

There was no answer. Suddenly worried, Vledder ran up the stairs. His fears were unfounded. He found DeKok in the bedroom with the dead woman. He was seated on a fragile looking chair in front of the make-up table. The contents of a medicine chest had been spread out before him. Silently he pointed at a number of ampules.

Vledder looked closely.

"Insulin."

DeKok nodded.

"And old Mrs. Weer was not diabetic."

"She wasn't?"

"No," repeated DeKok patiently, "she didn't need insulin."

* * *

DeKok leaned with his back against a wall of books in the dark library of villa *Jolanda*. Above him, in the bedroom of the old lady, the fingerprint experts and the photographer and all the other forensic and technical experts that were usually called to the scene of a murder, were busily completing their macabre business under the watchful eyes of young Vledder. Across from him, a bit off to the side, was Jerome. It was as if DeKok saw the man for the first time. During their last meeting, in the office of the Commissaris, the mother had so clearly dominated the gathering that Jerome had faded in the background of the attention that had been aimed at her forceful personality. For the first time DeKok discovered the broad chin, the sharp lines around the mouth, the wide nostrils and the watchful look in the hard, blue eyes.

"You confronted me rather abruptly with my mother's death." Jerome's voice was bitter, accusing. "If this is a sample of your *tactics*, I can't exactly admire it. I would have expected that you would have prepared me, warned me in some way."

DeKok looked at him without an expression on his face.

"Forgive me," he said in an apologetic tone that was not matched by the expression on his face. "I didn't expect you to be shocked."

Jerome's eyes became slits.

"What's that supposed to mean? A stupid expectation, I'd say. Don't you think so yourself? After all, she *is* my mother."

DeKok nodded vaguely.

"A remarkable woman. Admirable. So, you hadn't expected her death?"

Jerome gestured wildly.

"Of course I hadn't expected her death. Not this suddenly, anyway. There was nothing wrong with Mother. I mean, she wasn't sick, or anything. She was in very good physical shape for her age. Mentally she was also still very much alert."

DeKok sighed deeply.

"That must have been it," he said thoughtfully.

"I don't understand you."

For a moment Jerome was startled by DeKok's eyebrows. They seemed to jump clear off his forehead and then, just as quickly, subsided.

"Her mental alertness," he explained. Jerome forgot about the eyebrows. "You see," continued DeKok, "I was certain that she knew exactly who had killed Juliette . . . and why."

Jerome laughed foolishly, a short, nervous laughter.

"But then she would have said so this morning. To you . . . to me, to the Commissaris."

DeKok rubbed the bridge of his nose with a little finger.

"Your mother," he drawled, "was an intelligent woman. I think she wanted to be sure, did not want to make unsubstantiated accusations. Something must have been lacking. She might have been looking for corroborating proof."

Jerome looked at him with disbelief on his face.

"Proof?"

DeKok nodded.

"Some facet, a hint, something that she would have liked to include as proof, as confirmation."

"You mean a missing link, something she would find before eight o'clock tonight?"

DeKok grinned without joy. The grin had nothing of the boyish grin of genuine pleasure that sometimes lit up his face. It was more a grimace than a grin.

"Very good," he said with well-feigned admiration in his voice. "And the murderer was sufficiently convinced that she would find the missing link that he was not prepared to take the risk of letting her live beyond eight o'clock."

He walked away from the bookshelves and sank down in an easy chair across from Jerome. He looked at the other man. His sharp scrutiny registered every nuance, each change of expression.

"You knew," accused DeKok, "that your mother had an appointment with us at eight o'clock."

Jerome looked back, outwardly unmoved.

"I knew," he answered resignedly. "After all, I was there when she made the appointment with you. It's useless to deny it." He paused, brought both hands forward and rested the fingertips against each other. "But let me tell you something, Inspector.

Nobody mourns Mother's passing more than I. She was my support, my advisor, as she was the support and advisor for my father. Believe me, CIH owes its growth, its importance to her. She was the one who inspired my father, the brain behind his deeds. When the old man died, nothing changed. I succeeded him . . . took over as the new puppet on the strings of my mother. Perhaps this sounds cynical to you, but it isn't meant that way. Mother had an infallible instinct for business. Every movement in the Stock Market, every deviation in the exchange rate, they had no secrets for her. Her analysis was always precise, accurate and effective. It would have been stupid to go against her advice."

"Did she have enemies?"

A shadow fled across Jerome's face.

"Mother's role was well known in the inner circles of CIH. Cartoons about her circulated with some frequency. She would be depicted as a lion tamer, allowing old Henry to roar only on command. What I mean to say . . . not everybody admired her. She has broken careers, stopped others from reaching the top. I know some who speak her name with hate and with loathing." He smiled, a tired, wan smile. "You must realize that through my father she was the actual power at CIH. She decided the fate of every employee, from the janitor to the members of the Board of Directors."

"A remarkable woman," praised DeKok.

Jerome nodded.

"A remarkable woman," he repeated thoughtfully.

"You're the oldest son?"

"No . . . not me. Jonathan . . . Jonathan is older."

"Why isn't he in the business?"

Jerome's face fell, became more introspective.

"Father wanted Jonathan to succeed him."

DeKok gave him a long, searching look.

"Mother was against it?"

Jerome nodded slowly, reluctantly.

"Although Jonathan was the oldest, had first right of refusal, so to speak, Mother did not find him suitable. In her eyes Jonathan was too unwilling, too stubborn . . . too unpredictable."

"Not a puppet on a string?" DeKok's voice was devoid of any intonation. It was flat, even, stating a fact, rather than asking a question.

But Jerome reacted immediately. Sharply he looked up. An angry gleam flickered in his hard, blue eyes and for a moment it seemed as if he would say, or do, something he might regret. Then, with an effort, he controlled himself. It happened so fast that if DeKok had not been watching him closely, he might have lost the by-play altogether.

"Mother had little contact with Jonathan," he said calmly, outwardly relaxed. "They did not understand each other . . . or did not *want* to understand each other. They couldn't be in the same room for more than a few minutes without disagreeing about something. It was almost open hostility."

DeKok nodded his understanding.

"Did Jonathan know that his father had picked him as successor?"

Jerome nodded vehemently.

"Oh, yes. From an early age. There was never any doubt about that. In many ways father was an eccentric. Perhaps you've noticed that he had a preference for the letter 'J'? The estate is called *Jolanda*, the yacht was named *Julia* and he picked *Jonathan*, *Jerome* and *Juliette* for the names of his children. Father loved his oldest son very much. Jonathan means 'Jawheh's gift'. Father always considered the fact that his first-born was a son as a gift from the gods. Jonathan's succession in the business was probably the only point on which the old man would never have capitulated."

DeKok looked surprised.

"But you wound up in charge."

Jerome rubbed his cheeks, as if trying to restore circulation.

"Indeed," he said dully. "I became Chief Executive Officer at CIH. Come to think of it, a rather incomprehensible sequence of events. Even for me."

"How's that?"

"When father suddenly died aboard *Julia*, it turned out that there wasn't a single document that dealt with the succession. There wasn't even a valid Last Will and Testament. Because of that, Mother became the major shareholder, virtually overnight."

DeKok looked at him.

"And Mother ignored old Henry's wishes and named you as Chief Executive Officer."

Jerome sighed deeply.

"That's what happened all right. It's painful for me to have to tell you all of this. When Jonathan heard that I, not he, would be in charge of the Company after father's death, he was, to say the least, very upset. He cursed Mother and called her an old witch and accused both her and me of forgery, of suppressing documents. It was a terrible scene."

He paused, reliving the moments. DeKok waited patiently.

"I can safely say," continued Jerome Weer, "that Jonathan acted crazy. He could not have been responsible for what he said. He literally foamed at the mouth. Juliette and I could barely keep him under control. We had to forcibly restrain him. Later . . . much later, he calmed down and was able to participate normally in the conversation."

Again he paused. He rubbed his eyes in a tired gesture and sighed deeply. After a while he went on.

"There was a lot to take care of. A lot of details. Father had only been dead for hours and his sudden death caused a lot of problems. That's one of the reasons Mother wanted to settle the matter of succession at once." He shook his head. "For a while we believed that Jonathan had resigned himself to the situation, but when we gathered one more time around the body of the old man, before we left the boat, he suddenly placed his hand on the old man's chest and he swore . . ."

Suddenly he stopped talking. He hung his head in silence. His mouth sagged and all blood drained from his face.

After a while, DeKok moved his chair a bit closer.

"What did he swear?"

Jerome swallowed.

"He swore that he would kill us all . . . one by one."

10

Vledder approached DeKok's desk, balancing two nearly overflowing coffee mugs and placed one in front of DeKok. With a sigh he quickly shifted his grip on the other mug in order to take it by the cool handle.

"A theatrical gesture," said Vledder.

DeKok smiled mischievously.

"The coffee?"

"No, the oath at the deathbed."

DeKok's face became serious.

"Theatrical and . . . sinister."

Vledder nodded.

"If Jonathan Weer is engaged in systematically wiping out his family, we'd better arrest him as soon as possible."

DeKok pulled on his lower lip and let it plop back. Then he picked up the mug and slurped comfortably. He leaned back and seemed to savor the coffee as if it was one of his favorite cognacs. His face became thoughtful.

"If Jonathan . . ." he said at last, not completing the sentence.

Vledder gave him a searching look.

"You don't believe it?"

DeKok shrugged his shoulders.

"I don't know," he said, irritation in his voice. "I can't rid myself of the idea that there's more here than meets the eye. There's no pattern, it's all too obscure."

Vledder was astonished.

"Obscure?" he repeated. "How can you say that! There's a clear connection between the two killings. I mean, Jonathan swore aboard *Julia* that he would kill his family, one by one. Well, Juliette and the old lady were both aboard at the time and now they're both dead. In both cases the killer was as careful as could be."

DeKok looked at him from over the rim of his mug.

"Careful?"

"There wasn't a fingerprint to be found in the bedroom. Nothing, not even a fragment. Not even a fragment belonging to the deceased. Everything, and I mean *everything*, had been meticulously cleaned. All the little jars on the dressing table, and there must have been more than three dozen, were all carefully wiped clean."

"What about the window . . . the broken window downstairs?"

Vledder grinned broadly.

"Everything in that little office had been wiped, every drawer, every leg on both chairs, I tell you, *everything!*"

DeKok did not react. Pensively he stared at nothing at all, taking a slurp from his coffee at irregular intervals. Then he leaned forward and rested both elbows on the edge of the desk. His broad face, marked by the lines of a good-natured boxer had a vacant look. But behind the inexpressive semblance his brain worked at top speed, looking at aspects of the case, turning them over in his mind and filing them back for future use. For the first time he became truly aware of the threat posed by the unknown opponent. How merciless the killer was . . . and could be.

"I'm not sure I can find the words," he said after a long interval, "but this case suffocates me. Both killings seemed to have been performed so casually, so emotionless. Almost inhuman. It looks like the work of a professional killer."

He looked at Vledder who had started to play with the keyboard of his computer.

"What did the coroner say?"

Vledder shook his head.

"Dr. Koning was vague and non-committal, as always."

"I wonder if that man ever sleeps," said DeKok idly.

"What?"

"Nothing, Did you show him the ampules?"

"Yes."

"Well, what did he say about them."

"Nothing, just insulin ampules. Nothing remarkable about them. But he did say what you said ... Mrs. Weer wasn't a diabetic."

DeKok smiled.

"He must have seen what I saw, or rather, noticed the same absence. No puncture marks on arms, or legs. You understand, from the needle?" He drained his coffee. "Did you find out about the servants?"

Vledder nodded again.

"A cleaning lady comes in five days a week. And there's an old man for the garden."

"Did you talk to them?"

Vledder spread his arms wide in a gesture of surrender.

"The cleaning lady is on vacation in Majorca and the gardener had his day off. Neighbors told me he visits his daughter in the provinces." DeKok smiled to himself. Vledder pronounced "provinces" the way a native Amsterdammer would, as if it were somewhere in impenetrable jungles, beyond ravines and other natural obstacles. Considering that Vledder had been born outside of Amsterdam, it was all the more remarkable. But Amsterdammers had a way of looking at the rest of Holland in the same way New Yorkers looked at the rest of the United States. While these thoughts went through his mind, he listened to Vledder.

"With the cooperation of the provincial police," continued Vledder, "I was able to talk to the old man. When I told him that Mrs. Weer was dead, he cried. He asked if Mrs. Padburgh had visited yet."

"Who's Mrs. Padburgh?"

"I'm not that far yet. You always insist on getting the details before I've had a chance to write them down."

"Sorry, but I like the sound of your voice. Go on."

"I haven't yet talked to Mrs. Padburgh. According to the gardener, she's a friend of old lady Weer. They used to visit in the afternoons. The two old ladies would drink tea together and gossip. Sometimes they played cribbage, or another of those old-fashioned games."

Vledder stopped talking. He rose to his feet and tossed his notebook on the desk.

"What do we care?" he asked emotionally. "What do we care whether a couple of old ladies waste the afternoon away playing cribbage. That doesn't bring us any closer to a solution. Dammit, DeKok, we have to *do* something. This is already the second killing!"

DeKok looked at him calmly.

"You count real good," he said laconically.

Vledder waved his arms, a red blush spread over his face.

"Well, how long can we let that go on?" he asked grimly, "Do we have to wait until Andrew Bearburgh and Brother Jerome have also been killed?"

DeKok ignored the outburst with sublime indifference. With a tired gesture he rubbed his eyes.

"Alright already," he said finally. "Go on and send an APB: Location, apprehension and incarceration of one Jonathan Weer."

"On what charge?"

DeKok sighed, a resigned look on his face.

"Murder . . . multiple murder," he said.

* * *

DeKok bowed with old-world charm and took his hat off with a graceful gesture, reminiscent of an earlier age.

"Mrs. Padburgh?"

"Yes?"

"My name is DeKok . . . with, eh, with kay-oh-kay." He pointed at Vledder. "Allow me to introduce my colleague, Inspector Vledder. We're from Homicide."

"Homicide?"

"Indeed, we're assigned to the Warmoes Street station and we would like to ask you a few questions. May we enter?"

Mrs. Padburgh nodded.

"Please do," she said diffidently.

She opened wide the front door and preceded the two policemen toward a cozy living room.

"Please be seated, gentlemen." She pointed at some easy chairs. "Please tell me how I can help you?"

DeKok hesitated momentarily. Then he took the plunge.

"You know Mrs. Weer?"

"Oh, yes."

"You visited her this afternoon?"

"No, not this afternoon."

DeKok coughed discreetly.

"But you normally visit each other in the afternoon?"

Mrs. Padburgh looked from DeKok to Vledder and back to DeKok. An uneasy look came into her brown eyes.

"Why do you ask?" she asked. "Is something the matter?"

DeKok nodded gravely.

"We found her," he said solemnly, "dead in her bed."

Mrs. Padburgh raised a hand to her mouth as her eyes widened.

"Heart attack?"

DeKok shook his head.

"Murder."

She stared at DeKok with eyes that refused to believe at first. But slowly realization overwhelmed her.

"Mur . . . murdered?" she stuttered. "B-bu . . . but that's, that's terrible. Her too? You know about her daughter, don't you? When did it happen?"

"In the course of the afternoon."

"Then it must have been after two o'clock."

"After two o'clock?"

"Certainly. At about that time I spoke with her on the telephone. She called me to apologize for not being able to see me today. She was expecting visitors."

"What . . . what kind of visitors?"

Mrs. Padburgh seemed confused.

"She didn't say. She seemed rather upset. She asked if I had seen the articles about Juliette, in the papers. Well, in connection with that she had an appointment with some Inspectors from the police and she . . ."

DeKok waved her into silence.

"What did she say about the visitors in the afternoon?"

She shook her head, unsure of herself.

"Nothing. We didn't talk about that at all. We didn't talk that long, anyway. The conversation was practically over before it began because she was in a hurry. She still had to look something up, she said."

"What?"

"I don't know that."

DeKok leaned toward her.

"You're considered to be her friend," he said affably. "Did she ever mention anything confidential, something that might be of use to us in our investigations?"

The friendly face of Mrs. Padburgh looked woebegone.

"We never talked a lot. That is, we didn't talk as much as female friends are supposed to be doing, women together, don't you know? Our conversations were more ... more business-like."

"You didn't work for her?"

Mrs Padburgh smiled shyly. The idea seemed to amuse her.

"No ... no, happily not."

DeKok looked at her intently.

"Happily ... not? Is that what you said?"

Mrs. Padburgh again regained her countenance. She looked serious.

"She wasn't ... she wasn't an easy person to work for."

DeKok nodded understanding.

"Of course, I understand. How often did she visit you? I mean, your visits were reciprocated, weren't they?"

"Sometimes, yes, but not often. She preferred to stay in her own home."

"Are you diabetic?"

Mrs. Padburgh looked at him in astonishment.

"How did you know?"

DeKok gave her a winning smile.

"I didn't *know*," he said easily, "I just guessed." He waved the subject into unimportance. "Tell me about Mrs. Weer?" he demanded.

Mrs. Padburgh sighed long and deeply.

"There's so much to tell about her. Mrs. Weer was a dynamic woman and, despite her years, gifted with a cool, sharp analytical mind. Attributes for which I admired her. Compared to her, I'm just another old lady. My husband, God rest his soul, used to say . . ."

DeKok ruthlessly stemmed the flow of words.

"Did she ever talk about her children?"

Mrs. Padburgh appeared to be lost in thought. Then she spoke.

"Sometimes she lamented the fact that her children didn't take after her more. Jerome is the only one who looks like me, she used to say."

"What about Jonathan?"

Mrs. Padburgh smiled, almost tenderly.

"Jonathan and Juliette . . . she always mentioned them in the same breath, *devilish creatures in which the voluptuous genes of the Weers have found a fertile soil.*" She smiled again, apologetic. "I quote her verbatim," she explained.

DeKok laughed.

"That bad, eh?"

Mrs. Padburgh closed her eyes momentarily and nodded, slowly, an indulgent look on her face.

"One could fill volumes with the love affairs of those two."

Vledder interrupted.

"Was she hard of hearing?" he asked suddenly.

"What . . . who?"

"Mrs. Weer."

"On the contrary, my old friend had extremely good hearing. I often was amazed by it. Sometimes she would remark, right in the middle of a conversation: 'Old Jacob is going home'. It was uncanny. She had no way of knowing, he was nowhere in

110

sight, but she could hear his footsteps on the gravel in the garden."

DeKok resumed the interrogation.

"Old Henry ... I mean, old *Mister* Weer ... he was healthy?"

"How do you mean?"

"Did he suffer from stomach ailments? Any other infirmities?"

Mrs. Padburgh shrugged her narrow shoulders. DeKok suddenly realized that the small-boned woman must have been an acknowledged beauty in her younger days. The helpless gesture, combined with the apologetic look in her eyes and the sad features on her face made it easy to imagine how young men must have flocked to her door. She would have mesmerized them.

"No," she said finally. "I don't think so. Sometimes he suffered from gall stones. He should really have been operated for that, but he resisted. If it was too bad, he would get a painkiller, an injection."

"That helped?"

"Yes, I suppose so. He almost never missed a day's work. The attacks never lasted very long, I think."

Again DeKok nodded understanding.

"Do you know Jan?"

She frowned prettily.

"You mean Jan Drunnen?"

"Yes, that's who I mean."

"I met him a few times."

"And?"

"You want to know what I think about him?"

"Exactly, if you please."

Mrs. Padburgh did not answer at once, her gaze wandered around the room. Then she looked at DeKok.

111

"He's very friendly, considerate, charming even . . ." She stopped, hesitated, looked for words. "But," she added after a long pause, "he's two-faced."

*　*　*

They drove back to the station, Vledder, as usual, at the wheel. DeKok detested driving. He was sprawled in the passenger seat, also as usual. His lower lip protruded slightly and almost met the brim of his little hat which had been pulled far forward. The greenish lights from the communication gear threw ghostly shadows on his craggy face.

"Did you alert Interpol?"

"Yes, Headquarters in Paris. They promised to spread the word, but suggested, and I agree, that they should concentrate in France. They especially alerted the police along the Riviera."

"All right, but it may be a waste of time. If Jonathan is indeed the man we're looking for, he's somewhere in Holland. Perhaps even in Amsterdam."

"But why?"

"In order to strike when possible, to keep a close eye on the comings and goings of his intended victims. His job isn't finished, you know."

Vledder absorbed the words in silence. In silence they drove on.

"If Jonathan didn't have a key," Vledder said suddenly, "why didn't he just ring the bell?"

DeKok lifted the brim of his hat a fraction of an inch and cast an eye at his partner.

"You're talking about the broken glass in the office, downstairs?"

"Yes." It sounded irritated. "I can't make it compute. I've been worrying about that problem since this afternoon."

"What exactly bothers you?"

Vledder glanced at him momentarily, but seemed reassured by DeKok's placid demeanor and the genuine interest in his voice. Vledder was not always sure of himself, especially around DeKok.

"Mrs. Weer expected visitors," he said, as if reciting a report. "Therefore she was awake. We found her dressed. The breaking of the glass in the office must have made some noise." He slapped his hand on the dashboard. "I checked the phones in the house myself. They worked just fine. Then, why didn't she call the police? She must have had plenty of time. She was alone, an old woman, alone in a big house. If somebody breaks your windows, it's only logical to call the police."

"Perhaps she didn't hear it."

Vledder grinned confidently.

"Aha, but Mrs. Padburgh just told us that there was nothing wrong with her hearing!" There was a note of triumph in his voice.

"Perhaps she didn't hear it," repeated DeKok softly.

"She was *not*, repeat *not*, hard of hearing." Vledder's tone had changed. Annoyance had been added to his sense of triumph.

DeKok scratched the back of his neck and yawned mightily.

"Tonight," he said calmly, "tonight, when you can't sleep anyway . . . think about it."

11

Commissaris Buitendam, the tall, stately chief of the Warmoes Street station walked toward DeKok with outstretched hand.

"Well done," he exclaimed. "Excellent work, I must say. You have solved both murders and in the shortest possible time. Congratulations!"

DeKok did not hide his astonishment.

"Solved?"

The Commissaris smiled.

"I read the telex report. The suspect is Jonathan, a brother, right?"

DeKok swallowed uneasily.

"The brother of Juliette, but the son of old Mrs. Weer," he explained.

The Commissaris smiled again, even wider.

"Excellent," he said, rubbing his hands together. "A very good job. I will also not stint my praise toward young Vledder, you may rest assured."

""Fine," responded DeKok.

The Commissaris nodded.

"I contacted the Judge-Advocate immediately after I read the message. Mr. Overcinge was extremely pleased."

DeKok took a close look at his chief. The face of his boss, the tone in which he spoke, all seemed suddenly unreal to DeKok. The reaction of the Commissaris was detached from reality, more on a political, a bureaucratic plane. A cruel, abstract atmosphere that was foreign to the gray sleuth. He would have liked to tell the Commissaris that celebrations were, to say the least, premature. Certainly celebrations were not in order based on the mere issuing of an APB for Jonathan Weer. It most definitely did *not* mean that the case was solved, that all questions had been answered. But he knew in his heart that it was useless. His fulsome, almost euphoric chief would wave away his objections, if he even heard them.

"Thank you," DeKok said simply and walked down the hall.

The Commissaris looked after him and shook his head.

* * *

"The Commissaris will-not-stint-his-praise toward you."

Vledder snorted.

"He won't stint what?"

DeKok smiled thinly.

"His praise. That's what he told me this morning. He had read the telex and concluded that all was solved."

Vledder shrugged his shoulder.

"So what?" he asked aggressively. "The boss is absolutely right. What else is left to do? As soon as we arrest Jonathan, he only has to confess and the case is closed."

DeKok scrutinized his young friend and wondered if he was joking. But Vledder's face was serious and he obviously believed what he said. Thoughtfully, DeKok pushed his lower lip forward.

"He only has to confess," he repeated tonelessly.

116

Vledder nodded emphatically.

"Exactly. That's it. Come, let me show you something." He took DeKok by the arm and led him to one of the interrogation rooms. "I asked him to wait here for a bit." He opened the door wide with a grandiose gesture. "Allow me to introduce you . . . Mr. Greenway, antiquarian."

DeKok's eyebrows vibrated slightly, but the famous ripple died aborning. He extended his hand.

"DeKok . . ."

". . . with kay-oh-kay," completed Vledder.

The antique dealer smiled politely.

"Greenway."

"You have something to tell us?"

"And something to show," answered Vledder happily. "Mr. Greenway came in about fifteen minutes ago. He asked for you, but you weren't here. Therefore he showed it to me."

"What?"

Greenway put his hand in his pocket and emerged with a small box.

"The police list was late this week," he apologized. "I only received it this morning. But after reading it, I came at once." He placed the box on the table and opened it with shaking fingers. "This should be it," he amplified.

DeKok leaned forward.

"The medallion!"

The antiquarian nodded.

"It tallies exactly with the description, see for yourself. An antique cameo, set in gold with an engraved flower pattern and red rubies."

DeKok looked up.

"How did you get it?"

"Bought it."

"Where?"

Mr. Greenway smiled shyly.

"I have a small shop in Deer Street. I specialize in antique jewelry. I'm well known in certain circles."

"Yes, yes," DeKok sounded impatient. "Who sold it to you?"

The antique dealer lifted his briefcase.

"Just to be on the safe side, I brought the register. It's been recorded on the twenty second."

DeKok accepted the register and leafed through it. When he found the twenty second of July, he made his finger travel down the column and read aloud:

"*Medallion, antique cameo, gold-leaf design setting, decorated with rubies, bought from . . .*" He looked at Vledder.

"Jonathan Weer," he added hoarsely.

The young inspector nodded complacently.

"Well," he added seriously, "it's pretty clear now. It's high time we intensify the search for brother Jonathan."

The antiquarian removed his glasses.

"He was a very nice man," he volunteered, "a real gentleman. He told me the medallion was an old family heirloom. It hurt him to be forced to part with it."

Vledder lost his temper. His face was red.

"It should have hurt him when he ripped it off," he said savagely.

Mr. Greenway looked at him with dismay.

"What do you mean?" The man sounded confused.

DeKok intervened hastily.

"Would you recognize him?"

Mr. Greenway stared into the distance.

"He wore dark glasses," he remarked pensively. "It *does* make it a bit more difficult." He smiled. "Still, if I saw the gentleman again . . ."

DeKok looked again at the register.

"There's no address here," he remarked.

The antique dealer made an apologetic gesture.

"The gentleman had no address, no regular address, he lived here and there, he said."

DeKok nodded his understanding.

"You wrote the purchase in yourself?"

"Oh, yes. At once."

"Did you recognize the name? Jonathan Weer? Is that what he told you? Did he spell it out for you?"

Greenway shook his head.

"No, no, no," he said indignantly. "No, I copied it from his passport. Yes, a valid passport."

* * *

Inspector DeKok played idly with the gold medallion, letting the gold chain ripple between his fingers and finally allowing it to swing from a finger. His thoughts were far away, exploring a labyrinth of facts, information, clues, hints and suppositions. It seemed that all clues and indications led to Jonathan. But who was Jonathan. A cold-blooded killer? A murdering maniac? What drove him, what motivated him? Revenge?

Vledder stood next to his desk and interrupted DeKok's thoughts.

"We'll have to start with his contacts."

DeKok grinned.

"Nice job for you. All those women he had affairs with . . ."

Vledder looked offended.

"What else can we do? It's our only chance at the moment. Nobody else is likely to tell us anything about the guy."

"Any results from the APB?"

Vledder shook his head sadly.

"Not a thing. Hotel police told us that Jonathan does not appear in their records. That's about it."

DeKok scratched the back of his neck.

"A meager harvest," he commiserated.

Vledder pressed his lips together. A stubborn, determined look made him look older than his years.

"We simply *must* find him," he said after a while, vehemence in his voice. "And as soon as possible. It's the only protection we can offer the others. Personally, I won't rest easy until we've got him under lock and key." He slapped his hand on DeKok's desk. "Dammit, DeKok, he's got to be *somewhere*! He can't have just disappeared. What about TV?"

DeKok shook his head.

"The Commissaris will never agree. Especially not in this case. Everybody is trying to contain the publicity as much as possible. The Weer name is too closely linked to CIH and that's too closely linked to a lot of important people, at least, the kind of people that don't like publicity."

"So, where does that leave us?"

DeKok rubbed his chin with a thoughtful gesture. A wicked gleam sparkled in his eyes.

"Perhaps . . . perhaps we can arrange a leak?"

"A leak?"

"Yes, why not?"

DeKok opened one of his desk drawers and took out a piece of paper. With large letters he wrote: *Where is Jonathan?* Using slightly smaller letters, he wrote underneath: *Will the vengeful son continue his lugubrious killing spree?* He held the sheet up for Vledder to see.

"What do you think?"

Vledder nodded in admiration.

"Sensational."

DeKok gestured toward the telephone.

120

"Why don't you see if some of your friends in the press are interested?"

"Then what?"

DeKok grinned infectiously.

"Oh well, you never know where a newspaper article might lead."

* * *

"Inspector DeKok?"

"Yes."

"You were interested in me?" The question sounded curt, cool, almost arrogant. "I understand that you have been inquiring after me."

DeKok gave the man an amused look.

"Perhaps if you introduced yourself?"

The man cleared his throat.

"My name is Drunnen . . . Jan Drunnen."

DeKok gave him a winning smile, friendly creases appeared around his mouth and were reflected in the wrinkles around his eyes. Meanwhile he studied the face of the man. His sharp gaze travelled from the sensuous, weak mouth to the light-brown, moist eyes and the slicked-down black hair. Red Tina, thought DeKok, was right. The dapper little chap gave a weak, somewhat soft impression.

"Please sit down." DeKok indicated the chair next to his desk. "How very nice of you to stop by."

Drunnen made a protesting gesture.

"I'm a busy man."

DeKok nodded sympathetic understanding, while managing to display an expression of awed gratitude.

"We won't keep you very long," he soothed. "But two terrible murders in less than twenty four hours ... we must investigate them thoroughly. I'm sure you understand."

Drunnen sighed a long-suffering sigh.

"I will, of course, cooperate with the authorities," he spoke resignedly. "Ask your questions."

DeKok took a deep breath, banished his irritation.

"I'm not your authority," he drawled. "Don't want to be, either. I'm your servant . . . a servant of the Law . . . your Law . . . everybody's Law. You understand? Your role of the 'persecuted' citizen is out of order and doesn't impress me."

Drunnen moved uneasily in his chair, suddenly aware of the hint of steel in the congenial exterior of the gray sleuth. The words, although spoken softly and without any special emphasis, had managed to convey an unspoken threat at complete variance with the mellow tone in which they had been uttered. Drunnen lost some of his arrogance.

"It's not pleasant to be involved in a murder investigation," he said, trying to regain his supercilious manner.

"Are you involved?" DeKok's voice was sharp.

Drunnen shrugged his shoulders reluctantly.

"I know the Weer family."

"Intimately?"

Drunnen nodded.

"You could say that. Indeed, intimately is the word. Old Mr. Henry Weer introduced me to the family. He liked me."

"You were his protege? He was your 'guru'?"

The young man grinned. It was not a pleasant grin.

"I know those terms are used in business, but I don't like them. Protege, guru, they have unpleasant connotations, don't you think? I prefer to think that Henry Weer appreciated my administrative qualities. Sounds a lot better, don't you agree?"

DeKok rubbed his face with both hands and looked at Drunnen from between his spread fingers.

"You ... eh, ... you had other qualities, besides administrative ... qualities?"

Drunnen became motionless. The weak mouth twitched momentarily and an angry look flickered in his eyes.

"What do you mean to imply?" he asked wearily.

DeKok made a vague, slow gesture.

"I was referring to your *amorous* qualities," he said with a hint of wonder in his voice. "After all, you'll have to admit that those, too, were highly appreciated."

Drunnen licked his dry lips.

"Old Henry wasn't that way."

DeKok looked up.

"But who was talking about Henry?" He smiled gently. "I meant Juliette."

Drunnen paled.

"There was nothing between Juliette and myself."

DeKok stood up and sighed deeply.

"It's silly to deny it." He placed a hand on the shoulder of the young man. "The two of you were a couple ... a good-looking couple ... an attention-grabbing couple. Slender, blonde Juliette and dark and handsome Jan Drunnen"

The young man shook his head stubbornly.

"There was nothing between us," he repeated.

DeKok sat down again.

"Would you like me," he said in a friendly tone of voice, "to call a few working girls from the Quarter who will, no doubt, recognize you at once? Believe me, they will swear under oath that they've seen you many, many times with Juliette." He paused for effect. "Or do you think that Slate Makers Alley is too close to Old Church Square for comfort?"

Drunnen's reaction was emphatic.

123

"I had nothing to do with her death." He jumped from his chair and leaned over DeKok's desk, bringing his face close to that of the cop in a wild, almost threatening movement. "I didn't kill her, you hear me, I didn't kill her!"

DeKok, who had not moved during the outburst, now leaned back slightly and looked at Drunnen with a cold, searching, alert face.

"What was Juliette doing in the Red Light District?" he asked sharply.

Drunnen controlled himself, became calmer and sank back in his chair.

"We used to meet each other there."

"Where?"

"In St. John Street."

DeKok closed his eyes. It was as if a firecracker had gone off inside his head.

"St. John Street?" he repeated.

Drunnen gave a tired nod.

"Jonathan has a house there."

12

"Pretty stupid, in retrospect. Immediately after discovering the corpse we should have done a house-to-house in the neighborhood."

DeKok nodded quietly.

"I was thinking the same, just now."

Irritated, Vledder shook his head.

"But who would suspect it?" he exclaimed. "It's just too absurd. What sort of killer puts the body of the victim on his own doorstep?"

DeKok sighed.

"And it remains to be seen if we would have found out much with a house-to-house. We probably would have passed it by."

"Why's that?"

"According to Drunnen there was almost never anybody home. It was only occupied when Jonathan happened to stay in Amsterdam for a few days. Anyway, the connection with Jonathan Weer wouldn't be that easy to make. I called the city registry and 137 St. John Street is not in his name. He's also not registered at that address."

"Who is?"

"Some real estate broker."

Vledder frowned.

"Why so secretive?"

"According to Drunnen, Jonathan didn't want the address known. He considered the house a hideaway, a place where he could be anonymous. He only received his most intimate friends there."

"Women?"

"Those too."

"Then . . . what was Juliette doing there?"

DeKok smiled.

"She had a key. Jonathan allowed her the use of the house whenever she wanted."

Vledder grinned.

"Aha, so *that* was the love-nest. That's were she took her lovers . . . including Drunnen."

DeKok grimaced.

"If we can believe Mrs. Padburgh . . . many, many lovers."

Vledder stared pensively at nothing at all.

"Now it also becomes clear why she didn't have herself driven to the place of the appointment, but why she got out of the car in front of the hotel. The last thing she wanted was that jealous Andrew would find out about the address."

DeKok nodded seriously.

"She didn't walk," he said sadly, "but *ran* toward her death." He rose from his chair and ambled over to the coat rack. "I think we should go take a look." He hesitated for a moment. "Bring a good flashlight and don't forget your cuffs. You never know, he just might be hiding out there."

Vledder looked surprised.

"Who . . . Jonathan?"

"Yes."

Vledder grinned unpleasantly.

"He'd have to be crazy!"

DeKok gave him a long, hard stare.

"That," he said slowly, "is what I'm wondering about."

* * *

The house at 137 St. John Street turned out to be small, low and apparently neglected. It was situated on the corner of Slate Maker Alley and presented small, dirty windows and a front door marked by peeling paint. Some of the bricks were crumbling and the entire facade leaned tiredly forward.

Vledder glanced up at the front of the house.

"Little more than a shack," he said with contempt in his voice. "I don't think it's been used for some time."

DeKok moved his hand along the door lintels.

"It's deceptive," he remarked softly. "The house is most certainly used on a regular basis. The hinges and the lock are well oiled and the lock looks formidable." He pressed down on the old-fashioned door handle, but the door was securely locked.

"You have a key?"

DeKok shook his head.

"Jan Drunnen never had a key to the house and the killer must have taken the key from Juliette's purse. There was no key in her purse that could have fitted in this lock." His face was transformed by a broad grin. "However," he added, "I always have Handy Henkie's little gift to baffled policemen." His hand went into a pocket, looking for the ingenious invention of the ex-burglar.

Vledder sighed demonstratively.

"That's illegal search and seizure, you know." He shook his head. "You can't trample the Law like that, one of these days you're going to get in real trouble."

DeKok smiled gently.

"But not today," he said carelessly. "And tomorrow . . . tomorrow can take care of itself. You know, my old mother always used to say: *Son* . . . she called me Son . . . *Son, people suffer most from the fear they anticipate.*"

Vledder snorted.

"Perhaps. You had a wise mother, but what did she mean by that?"

"Well, the way she explained it, half the things you worry about never happen and the rest . . . the rest, you find a solution when the time comes."

"By that reasoning you never have to worry about anything."

DeKok nodded agreement.

"You're right. Mother tackled life with a battery of old sayings and Bible texts. It worked for her. I always admired her for it. Her most favorite . . ."

Vledder poked him lightly with an elbow.

"Later. Just get a move on. If you take much longer, we'll be performing in front of a mob."

DeKok wiped the sweat from his brow, while he adjusted something on the instrument in his hand.

"You're right," he said. "But this is an old lock. I don't think Henkie ever figured on me having to open one like this. The thing may date back to Napoleon. Maybe this will be Henkie's Waterloo."

"Well, at least it has something in common with your favorite beverage," joked Vledder, but with tension in his voice.

DeKok continued to worry the lock. Progress was indeed a lot less smooth than under previous, similar circumstances. As the time required to open the lock increased, DeKok became more nervous, more tense. His usually so sensitive fingertips seemed to slip past the right pressure points as if they did not exist. With an effort he controlled himself, took a deep breath and then, with a last, final click, the lock yielded. Softly he again pushed down on the old fashioned door handle. Without effort and soundlessly on its oiled hinges, the door opened wider.

"Step aside," he whispered. "You never know who's waiting for us."

He gave the door a sudden push and silently it opened wide. For a few seconds the two Inspectors waited breathlessly, one on either side of the door. Nothing happened. Vledder whipped inside, fast, agile, cat-like. DeKok followed, slower, more careful.

* * *

It took a while before their eyes adjusted to the gloom inside. Slowly the interior took form. Softly Vledder closed the front door behind them and played the light of his flashlight over the room. It was strangely decorated. Expensive Persian carpets covered the floor and the walls. Turkish and Moroccan items served as focal points for large numbers of bearskins in several colors, leather hassocks and innumerable pillows embroidered with strange, vivid designs. The unmistakable smell of incense added to the bizarre atmosphere.

"Sheik Jonathan," mocked Vledder.

DeKok ignored the remark. Carefully he stepped further into the strange room. Amsterdam houses were usually narrow, tall and deep. Some were even wedge-shaped because taxes used to be assessed based on the width of the house that fronted the street. But this house was neither high, nor deep. A bamboo curtain separated the Oriental front room from a small, ultra modern, very western kitchen. The kitchen looked out on a minuscule backyard. Just behind the curtain a metal circular stairway led upstairs.

DeKok looked around. The kitchen was spotlessly clean with the aseptic, yet homey appearance that only a Dutch kitchen seems to be able to reflect. Even the grout between the white floor tiles had the same color as the tiles. In contrast to the dirty windows in the front, all the glass work in the kitchen gleamed as if it had been cleaned only minutes ago. After a last look around the kitchen, without touching anything, DeKok turned toward the staircase.

Slowly he climbed the curving stairs. There was a hatch at the top of the stairs. Careful, prepared for every eventuality, DeKok pushed up. Nothing happened. Slowly he opened the hatch all the way. The hatch opened into a bedroom with a thick, white carpet, an enormous bed and downy pillows. Toward the rear, above the kitchen, was a miniature bathroom in an antique style with a lot of pink and gold. The old-fashioned, claw-footed tub took up most of the space.

He looked around for a while and descended again to the floor below.

He found young Vledder in the Oriental room, perched on a stack of pillows with a notebook on his knees. A diffused light burned somewhere in the gloom of the ceiling, casting just enough light to illuminate the shadows without the power to banish them.

"Nothing, nobody upstairs," reported DeKok. "And everything has been cleaned."

Vledder looked up.

"Our careful killer," he said bitterly, "has again wiped out all traces. You can't even smell anything. Everything stinks of incense, the place smells like a Buddhist monastery."

DeKok nodded.

"No chairs or couches either," he remarked.

"Jonathan," said Vledder with a mocking smile, "lived close to the ground. It's just pelts and pillows. He must have spent his time here almost exclusively in a prone position."

"Supine," corrected DeKok absent-mindedly.

"Huh?"

"On his back, lying down . . ." With a bored look on his face, DeKok paced through the room and moodily kicked a few pillows into a corner. "Well, there's nothing else here for us," he said with obvious displeasure. "You have any bright ideas?"

Vledder tapped his notebook with his pen.

"I made a few notes," he offered.

"What about?"

"Juliette's murder. When we reconstruct the case, we arrive at the following scenario." He coughed diffidently. "Jonathan Weer delivers, or causes to be delivered, a letter to the house on the Mirror's Canal. In the letter he invites Juliette to visit him here, in St. John Street, at eight o'clock that night. The fact that the letter has been removed from the envelope is an indication of that. Juliette responds unsuspectingly and after her dinner date with Andrew, has herself driven to Hotel Krasnapolsky. From that point she walks to this house, where her murderer waits for her. Jonathan strangles her and waits calmly until it's dark enough outside to place the body around the corner in Slate Makers Alley. The next day he sells the medallion he ripped from around her neck to Greenway in Deer Street and identifies himself with his passport." With a self-satisfied look on his face, Vledder closed his notebook and looked at his mentor. "Well, what do you think?"

DeKok pursed his lips.

"It *sounds* convincing."

Vledder rose from his stack of cushions, tried to find the hidden meaning behind DeKok's expression. There had been a definite tone in the voice of the older man that alerted him, brought him up short.

"Is . . . is there something wrong with it?"

DeKok looked at him with an expressionless face.

"It sounds convincing," he repeated. "You could transfer it almost literally to an official report." He turned and walked toward the door. "Come on, let's go. Put everything back the way we found it and turn the lights off. Maybe he'll be back."

Vledder pushed a hassock closer to the wall, spread out the pillows he had piled up and retrieved the cushions DeKok had kicked aside. Then he straightened up and, turning off the light, followed DeKok reluctantly.

"You don't agree?" he asked hesitatingly, unsure of himself.

DeKok did not answer. He looked at his watch.

"My wife promised me a special fondue tonight, with fresh, homemade bread and an excellent bottle of Bordeaux."

"You mean . . . you're going home?"

DeKok smiled gently.

"It's been enough for one day. If you have some time tomorrow, find out where *Julia* is docked and find the address of the parents of the drowned sailor."

"John Peter Opperman?"

"Exactly, I'd like to talk to them."

Vledder cast him a suspicious look.

"And what will you be doing, tomorrow?"

DeKok closed the door behind them and locked it in less time than he had used to open it.

"Tomorrow, Juliette and her Mother are being buried at Sorrow Field."

"And you're going?"

DeKok nodded gravely.

"I'm crazy about funerals."

* * *

"Mother and daughter ... both felled by the cruel hand of a murderer." The voice of the old minister carried easily through the vaulted space of the Chapel. "We beg you, oh Lord, that both will be received by you to bask in the glory of your mercy."

"And what about the killer?" whispered DeKok.

Jerome Weer looked aside, shock and surprise on his face.

"Does he deserve God's mercy?"

DeKok leaned closer.

"Don't you think so?" DeKok's voice was low, but the question was insistent.

Jerome swallowed. His face turned a deep red with indignation.

"Let the vials of ..." he began, but did not complete the sentence.

DeKok was enough of a puritan to understand the allusion.

"Let the vials of wrath be poured out upon him," he lisped.

Jerome nodded with compressed lips and a determined look on his face.

The minister ended the prayer. His "Amen!" bounced off the walls and was repeated by the audience until it rolled away into an indistinguishable murmur that was eventually drowned by the first chords of the organ.

With the first tones of the organ, the minister walked away from the lectern with the stiff steps of an old man and moved to a side door. The audience listened in silence to the organ music and then the doors opened. A double row of professional pallbearers in old-fashioned tail coats and with veils descending from their top hats, approached the two coffins. With practiced ease the flower-bedecked coffins were hoisted upon their shoulders and, softly rocking in step with the pallbearers, the deceased were carried outside. Bright sunlight illuminated the coarse gravel on the path toward the grave as the visitors followed the coffins with subdued decorum.

DeKok separated himself from Jerome and found a place near the end of the procession. With half an eye he watched the next funeral party descending from the waiting cars and limousines. Another coffin slid out of the hearse and the Chapel was ready to perform the next rites. Not for the first time, DeKok reflected on this habit of having a non-denominational Chapel on the funeral grounds. It was certainly practical and probably cost-efficient as well. Both were virtues in the eyes of the stolid Dutch.

Diagonally in front of him, DeKok saw Andrew Bearburgh. The man walked with bowed head and did not seem part of the crowd. His gray hair, ruffled by the sultry breeze from between the tall, thin poplars that bordered the path, made him seem even more lost and alone among the many notables that followed the two coffins. DeKok recognized a member of the Amsterdam City Council, a number of directors of important concerns and an Under-Secretary from The Hague. Distinguished faces showing just the right amount of sorrow and introspection required by the occasion.

DeKok increased his pace and moved closer to Andrew. When the procession arrived at the grave, DeKok positioned himself behind Juliette's ex-husband and watched his reactions as the coffins were placed on the grave hoist. Andrew Bearburgh seemed unaffected.

Not until the two coffins slowly disappeared from sight did he break down. A tear dropped from his eyes and his adam's apple bobbed up and down. His mouth moved. "Adieu, Juliette." He said more, but DeKok withdrew discreetly. His feeling of propriety, of piety, left him no other choice. He moved against his will but in almost the same instance he regretted the impulse and again started to move closer.

The Under-Secretary spoke compassionate words with a cool and experienced air about him. DeKok's sensibilities were insulted. He hated cliches and hollow phrases at moments like this. He much preferred raw emotions. At least they were honest.

The ceremonies at the grave site concluded with a word of thanks from Jerome on behalf of the family and the crowd dispersed.

Andrew Bearburgh glanced aside and seemed to notice DeKok for the first time.

"You're here too?" There was surprise in his voice.

"As a sign of respect," admitted DeKok seriously.

Andrew bowed his head.

"I didn't want all this," he said softly.

DeKok looked at him.

"What didn't you want?"

"This double funeral, this . . . this spectacle. I had wanted to bury Juliette by herself, by myself. You understand, without all these people. I would have liked to say my farewells privately. Far away, somewhere in a small cemetery."

"What happened?"

"Mighty CIH would not allow it."

"You mean, of course, *Jerome* did not allow it."

Bearburgh snorted his disgust.

"She had to be buried next to her mother. United in death he called it." Sadly he shook his head. "Juliette never loved her mother. Sometimes I thought that she only married me in order to get away from the old witch, to be free of the conniving snake."

"Sounds hard."

Andrew Bearburgh nodded, but there was no remorse in his voice when he spoke.

"Yes, I should keep quiet about it. It's against the code, you know, nothing but good about the dead and all that . . . . Yes, even if they poisoned the lives of others, speak no evil of the dead."

They walked along in silence. After a while DeKok gestured vaguely around.

"I didn't see Jonathan," he remarked casually.

An ugly smile played around Andrew's lips.

"I hope he strikes again, soon."

DeKok looked at him with narrowed eyes.

"Jonathan?" he asked.

"Yes, of course, Jonathan."

"But aren't *you* worried?"

Andrew looked at him, genuine surprise on his guileless face.

"But I have nothing to worry about."

With an effort DeKok remained expressionless.

"Who does?"

"Jerome . . . he is a Weer."

13

Commissaris Buitendam looked wrathful. His eyebrows, although not having the remotest chance of imitating DeKok's amazing gymnastics with that part of the anatomy, fairly bristled and his nostrils quivered in anger. With jerky movements, evidence of his attempt to control himself, he slapped a newspaper down on the desk.

"That's your handiwork," he accused.

DeKok beheld his chief with artless confusion.

"What is my handiwork?"

The Commissaris turned the paper toward him and DeKok read the headlines in a loud voice.

"WILL THE VENGEFUL SON CONTINUE HIS GRISLY MURDERS! WHERE'S JONATHAN?" He looked at his chief with a grin on his face. "That's supposed to be *my* handiwork?"

The Commissaris almost rose from his chair.

"Yes," he hissed, "You've provided this information, this . . . these . . . these stories to the press."

With an innocent face, DeKok tapped himself on the chest.

"But I don't work for the press," he refuted.

The Commissaris shook his head, as if trying to clear it.

"NO," he roared, "you *don't* work for the press, you're supposed to be working for the police! And that means, among other things, that you're supposed to keep certain things confidential! They are really upset about this newspaper report, let me tell you!"

DeKok's face became expressionless.

"Who are *they*?" he asked sharply.

The Commissaris reacted with unabated anger.

"That's none of your damned business. That's *my* business. You'll hear more about this. This is not the end of this, I can promise you."

DeKok shook his head slowly, pityingly.

"The APB for Jonathan over which *they* were so excited and pleased," he began, sarcasm dripping from every syllable, "appeared in every police station and border post. Even Interpol is aware. It should be a matter of routine to get a copy of it. Any journalist worth his salt . . ." He did not complete the sentence, but smiled politely. "Well, when you've found the so-called *leak*, I'm sure you'll let me know."

The commissarial face had paled. He gripped the edge of his desk with one hand and stretched the other hand out toward the door.

"OUT!" he roared.

DeKok left.

* * *

"How was the funeral?" Vledder was just coming up the stairs when he saw DeKok in the corridor.

DeKok shrugged his shoulders at the question.

"The usual. Nothing out of the ordinary. There *was* quite a bit of interest, as was to be expected. After all, the Weers are important people. But, also more or less as expected, Brother

Jonathan sparkled by his absence. Jerome was boring and obvious, Andrew was sad and discontented."

"Why was that?"

"Andrew wasn't too pleased with all the attention. He would have preferred to bury Juliette on his own, privately. 'In a small, intimate cemetery' were the words he used."

Vledder shook his head.

"Strange guy. You really believe he loved Juliette that much?"

DeKok stared at nothing in particular.

"The cloak of love," he pronounced, "is an all-encompassing shroud." It sounded ironic. After a while he continued: "Personally, I wouldn't be surprised at all, at all, if he killed her himself in a moment of unbridled passion."

"Seriously? A *crime passionnel*?"

DeKok nodded, a faraway look in his eyes.

"He told us that Juliette got out of the car in front of Krasnapolsky and from there he went straight home. But is it true? We have only his word for that. Nobody can either confirm, or deny, his story. What if, instead, he followed her to the house in St. John Street. A short exchange of words . . . flaring tempers . . . a strangle hold . . ."

Vledder seemed struck.

"But . . . but that's entirely possible," he uttered.

DeKok chewed his lower lip.

"But that's as far as I get, you see? I just can't find any way to fit him into the background of the other murders."

"Mrs. Weer and her husband."

DeKok sighed deeply.

"There's no motive for Andrew to be involved with them."

For a while the two inspectors stood next to each other in companionable silence, each occupied with his own thoughts.

"Did you see the Commissaris, by the way?" asked Vledder. "He was furious this morning, looking for you."

DeKok nodded vaguely.

"Yes, he wasn't too happy about the article in the newspaper."

Suddenly Vledder raised his hand to his forehead in a gesture of chagrin.

"Margo!" he cried out, visibly upset.

"Who's Margo?"

"She's waiting for you. She's been waiting for at least half an hour. She wants to file a complaint."

DeKok looked disgusted.

"A complaint?"

Vledder nodded.

"Yes, she wants to file a complaint against the newspaper. Because of that article."

DeKok scratched the back of his neck.

"Too bad," he mused, "I'm not a Catholic. *This* would be the proper time for a *Hail Mary*."

* * *

DeKok stood still, momentarily speechless. He looked at her with a long, appreciative look, undisguised admiration in his eyes.

"You're ... beautiful," he said with a suppressed sigh. "Exceedingly beautiful." He cocked his head at her, a slight smile around his lips. "You knew that already?"

She showed a row of small, white, even teeth and captivating dimples near the corners of her mouth.

"I've been told before," she said with a humorous glint in her eyes.

DeKok's face fell.

"I was afraid of that," he commented sadly.

She laughed freely.

"You're Inspector DeKok?"

" . . . with kay-oh-kay."

She laughed again.

"They told me you would say that."

DeKok made an apologetic gesture.

"I always want to make sure they spell my name right." He stole a glance at her short skirt as he slipped past her and sat down behind his desk.

"You're Margo?"

"Yes, Margo . . . Margo Stover."

DeKok pointed at the newspaper in her lap.

"And you're upset about something?"

A shadow fell across her face.

"Yes. I want to file a complaint. This is terrible." She unfolded the newspaper. "They're saying horrible things about Jonathan."

DeKok looked at her suspiciously.

"What sort of horrible things?"

She swallowed.

"It says, in so many words, that the police seriously suspect Jonathan of having killed his sister and his mother."

DeKok gave her a wan smile.

"The police have to take into consideration . . . have to consider all eventualities."

She nodded understandingly.

"But this is too absurd. Jonathan isn't like that at all. He wouldn't harm a fly, let alone kill his own mother and sister." She spoke rapidly, with a husky, emotional voice. "You *have* to be mistaken."

"Me?"

"Yes. You're in charge of the investigation. You're the one who circulated a request for . . . for apprehension."

"You're well informed."

She lowered her head.

"I went to the paper first. They gave me all the facts as they knew them and then suggested I talk to you."

DeKok pushed his chin further into the room.

"That's correct," he said, more sharply than he intended, "I've requested the apprehension of Jonathan Weer. On the basis of reasonable grounds, I assure you. And if Jonathan thinks that I'm wrong, then all he has to do is contact me to tell me so."

A pretty blush appeared on her cheeks.

"It's far beneath him to react to such absurd, scurrilous accusations."

DeKok leaned closer.

"How do you know?" he asked intently.

"I know him."

"Intimately?"

"That . . . that's none of your business."

"Did he send you?"

"No."

"Then, why are you here?"

Suddenly tears sprang into her eyes.

"It's mean," she sobbed. "It's just plain mean. Jonathan didn't do it. He did *not* commit those murders. Jonathan just isn't that way."

DeKok looked at her thoughtfully.

"Don't you agree yourself that it sounds just a little naive?"

She sighed deeply, fished a handkerchief from her purse and dried her tears.

"Well, *somebody* has to defend him," she pouted. "I know that Jonathan has a bad reputation, I'm well aware of the gossip that's being spread about him, believe me, I know. I also know that there have been a lot of women in his life, all kinds of women, married women . . ." She stopped, swallowed a lump in her throat, sighed deeply. "But that . . . that was *before* I knew him. Jonathan is a charming man with a life-style that many envy."

"A playboy?"

She reacted vehemently.

"But *not* a murderer!"

DeKok rose from his chair.

"You really believe in Jonathan's innocence?"

She looked up at him and nodded.

"Unconditionally?"

"Unconditionally!"

DeKok spread his arms wide.

"Tell me where I can find him."

She bowed her head. The long, blonde hair fell in front of her face and, from DeKok's vantage point, seemed to engulf her entire body.

DeKok came around the desk and took a chair across from her.

"Where can I find him?" he repeated gently.

She did not answer. She started to cry again. Her narrow shoulders shook and tears dripped on her lap.

For a long time DeKok looked at the huddled figure and he could not help feeling pity. Only a misanthrope, or somebody totally devoid of feeling could have remained unaffected by the obvious display of sorrow. And DeKok was neither. It was his nature to be sympathetic towards young women. He had a tendency to consider them as the daughters he had never had. In his experience young women, especially beautiful young women, seemed to have more than their fair share of trouble. He had often wondered about that. But then, he admitted to himself, his experience was probably colored by the fact that he was so close to the Red Light District, a cornucopia of beautiful, young women and, of course, in his work he seldom met anybody who was not in some sort of trouble.

He moved closer and touched her arm lightly.

"If Jonathan is innocent," he said in a friendly, fatherly tone of voice, "I will *prove* he's innocent. But I can only do that with his help. The facts, as we know them, are against him, you see? The longer he stays in hiding, the more difficult it becomes for all of us."

She raised a tear-stained face toward him.

"I don't know," she whispered, "I don't know where he is."

DeKok looked at her, a hint of suspicion in his eyes.

"You expect me to believe that?"

She nodded slowly, still sobbing.

"I haven't seen him for more than four weeks." With an enchanting, utterly feminine gesture she pushed the hair from her face and looked at him openly.

"I'm at wit's end, Mr. DeKok, believe me. I don't know what to do any more, what to think. I've been everywhere, looked everywhere. He's gone."

DeKok looked at her evenly.

"Another woman?"

A painful grimace was unable to distort the beauty of her face. She squared her shoulders.

"Oh, I can see how you would think that," she said bitterly. "Jonathan's past would certainly tempt you to think so. And I don't blame you for it, but it isn't that . . . not this time. Jonathan and I were about to be married."

DeKok's eyes narrowed slightly.

"Married?" he marvelled, "When?"

"This month."

"Where?"

"In Edam. It's such a nice town and they have a beautiful old Town Hall, from the 16th Century. We went by there once and Jonathan loved it. That's where we'll get married, he decided. We registered a few weeks later."

"Who was aware of your intended marriage?"

She shrugged her shoulders which did exciting things to the front of her blouse. Vledder looked interested, but Dekok did not seem to notice. Privately DeKok made a mental note to make sure that Vledder would be able to spend more time with Celine, his fiancee. It was time those two got married, too, thought DeKok.

"A few friends, acquaintances," answered Margo, unaware of the thoughts of the two men. "We wanted to keep it as private as possible."

"And your friends also don't know anything about Jonathan's whereabouts?"

She shook her head and sighed.

"I can understand how you can see a connection between Jonathan's disappearance and the death of Juliette and old Mrs. Weer. You're a policeman and you can't help but think that way." She looked at him. "And you're absolutely convinced that Jonathan is hiding from you?"

DeKok nodded seriously.

"If he's not hiding from me, who then?" He said it matter-of factly, but it sounded ironic.

A tortured look came over her.

"He isn't hiding from me, Mr. DeKok, if that's what you're implying . . . Jonathan and I love each other. It's just that simple. It wasn't a flirtation, or a sudden, momentary passion. We love each other deeply and we were going to be married . . . you understand? Until death do us part."

DeKok nodded slowly, as if he understood completely.

"Did he ever talk about his family?"

"Sometimes. When we were alone. When he needed to talk to someone he could trust."

"And?"

She closed her eyes, reflecting.

"After his father's death, Jonathan changed dramatically. He was less cheerful, less exuberant then before. Sometimes he was downright depressed, melancholy, somber. They killed the old man, he used to say, they didn't want me to get the business."

"Who's *they*?"

"The clique. That's what he called it. I always understood that 'the clique' included the entire Weer family with the exception of Jonathan."

DeKok smiled.

"He doesn't like his family?"

"No, not at all. He especially despises Andrew, his brother-in-law."

"Andrew Bearburgh?"

"Yes, he can't stand him. He maintains that Andrew married Juliette only for her money. Happily, apparently, old Henry figured that out real soon. He limited Juliette to a tight annuity and refused to take Andrew into the management of CIH. Andrew never forgave old Henry for that."

DeKok shrugged his shoulders carelessly.

"They're legally divorced. Andrew had nothing to gain from old Henry's death. There were no official ties."

Margo Stover looked at him sharply. The look in her clear, blue eyes was cold, observing.

"You're wrong. Andrew Bearburgh has a son."

14

DeKok paced up and down the large detective room, wildly gesticulating.

"Follow her," he ordered.

Vledder asked the obvious, superfluous question.

"Who?"

"Margo. Don't do it yourself. Let Dijk do it. You're too obvious, she'll recognize you."

Vledder located Robert Antoine Dijk behind one of the desks, grabbed him by an arm and urged him onto his feet while explaining what was needed.

DeKok watched them leave. He wanted to know where Margo was going, the intended spouse of the elusive Jonathan. His interview with the beautiful blonde had confused him, had served to neatly scrap most of his theories and suppositions. He seemed further away from a solution then before. In his mind he had already eliminated Andrew Bearburgh as a possible suspect. And now this petite blonde and, above all, exciting little creature came to tell him about Andrew's son. A completely legal son and offspring as a tangible result of his marriage to Juliette Weer. A son who was most certainly in line for an inheritance, a substantial inheritance. The only known grandson of old Henry and Mrs. Weer.

DeKok walked back to his desk and sat down. Perhaps, he thought, when you thought about it carefully, there *was* progress in the case. He slouched down in his chair and gave his thoughts free rein.

Andrew Bearburgh killed old Henry. It would not have been difficult for him to add something to the food aboard *Julia*, or to make sure that the old man ingested a lethal substance of some kind. The family's abhorrence of publicity worked in his favor and old Dr. Gelder was called in to declare a natural death. So far so good. There's no question of a will, or an allocation of inheritance. Old Mrs. Weer is still very much alive and becomes sole owner of the joint property of herself and her late husband. Including all the shares in CIH previously held by old Henry. The old lady, who is now in complete control of the company, assigns Jerome as Chief Executive Officer. Next Andrew kills Juliette. The picture changes. The power structure in CIH becomes more divided. Old Ms. Weer still has control, of course, but Jerome has some shares of his own . . . and Juliette's shares in the Company now, presumably, go to her son, her legal heir. DeKok grinned to himself. Temporary control of *that* part of the CIH stock will inevitably resort to the legal guardian of the young boy, his father, the aforementioned Andrew Bearburgh, a man of unblemished reputation and a fine and upstanding citizen. Then, if Mrs. Weer also dies . . . a portion of her estate would presumably be earmarked for her grandson . . ."

"Something funny?"

DeKok looked up. Ben Kruger, the fingerprint expert, stood in front of his desk. He had been so wrapped up in his thoughts and speculations that he had been unaware of his surroundings.

* * *

148

The old expert placed his briefcase on the desk and sat down.

"I've done quite a bit of work for you," he smirked.

"Work?" asked DeKok vaguely, his thoughts still far away.

"Yes. I still had that envelope from the purse of Juliette Weer. I used iodine vapors on it, but nothing happened. I do think it's an old envelope. It's heavily besmirched and the lines of dozens of prints criss-cross each other like a bowl of spaghetti. Hopeless."

DeKok looked at him with barely concealed amazement.

"You came all the way over here to tell me *that*?"

Kruger smiled secretively.

"I've something else for you." He took his briefcase and placed it on his knees. "After the murder of old Mrs. Weer, everything was again cleaned most meticulously."

"Yes, yes. Vledder told me that."

Kruger moved in his chair, opened his briefcase.

"There were some papers on the floor of the small office, downstairs. The one that was broken into."

"And you treated those with iodine vapors?"

Kruger nodded with a self-satisfied smile.

"I found some beautiful prints and I was able to make some very clear, detailed enlargements."

"You could have told me."

Kruger grinned and shook his head.

"That would have been useless. There are always fingerprints on papers . . . typists . . . secretaries . . . the man, or woman, who signs . . . the recipient. It all means nothing."

DeKok waited impassively.

"Go on."

Kruger looked disappointed.

"I've been able to do so very little for you in connection with these murders," he confessed. "But there was nothing, absolutely nothing and that bothered me. Therefore the papers.

Usually it's a wild goose chase, but I wanted to try. I went to the main office of CIH and asked Jerome Weer what sort of prints could reasonably expected to be on the papers."

"And?"

"He named old Mrs. Weer, of course, Henry Weer, some secretaries, an office boy, a Mr. Jan Drunnen and himself. Jerome Weer was extremely forthcoming. He did everything he could to help, very cooperative. So, I got prints of all concerned."

DeKok's eyebrows rippled and danced across his forehead. Kruger, who knew about the phenomenon, but had seldom seen it with his own eyes, was speechless. Not until the display subsided, did he realize what DeKok had said.

"But you never had the fingers of Mr. and Mrs. Weer," repeated DeKok.

Kruger laughed happily.

"But I did. During the investigation at villa 'Jolanda' I took the fingers of the corpse as a matter of course."

DeKok knew that "fingers" was the normal way in which cops spoke about fingerprints, but could not help thinking about Vledder, especially in the context in which Kruger had used the term. Vledder had told DeKok at one time that he had visions of Kruger moving around Amsterdam with a case full of severed fingers.

"What about Henry Weer?" he asked.

"Oh," answered Kruger, "I found them."

"You *found* them?"

Kruger looked very happy with himself.

"It wasn't difficult. You see, when you hold a letter, you get a distinct print of the thumb on the front of the sheet and vague impressions of the fingers on the back of the paper. Most of the papers were signed by Henry Weer himself. When people sign papers, they usually hold the sheet in place with the tips of the fingers of the other hand. To prevent it from shifting, you see.

Well, old Henry was no different. It took a few hours, but then I had all his prints."

DeKok rubbed the bridge of his nose with a little finger.

"Excellent, really excellent. But . . . what's the purpose?"

Kruger coughed discreetly.

"Well, I hoped to find prints of somebody in our own collection . . . some sort of burglar, you understand?"

DeKok smiled.

"And you didn't find that."

Kruger shook his head sadly.

"No, I didn't find that," he repeated slowly. "But I *did* find the prints of Jan Drunnen on all the papers. Very clear prints, as a matter of fact." He hesitated and then concluded: "Even on those papers that should not have been touched for at least thirty years or so, should not have left the house for whatever reason."

* * *

"Dijk is on her trail. He'll call as soon as he knows something. A remarkable girl like that, she should be easy to follow."

DeKok grinned.

"As long as she doesn't get into a fast car."

Vledder shrugged that away.

"We'd be out of luck. But what was the purpose of her visit?"

"You were here, you heard. She wanted us to know that she and Jonathan had wedding plans and she especially wanted us to know that Bearburgh had a son."

"I heard that, so what?"

DeKok pushed his lower lip forward. His face was serious.

"You obviously heard it, but you didn't think it through. That son is Juliette's legal heir."

151

"Dammit," he said spontaneously, "you're right. I hadn't realized that."

DeKok shook his head disapprovingly.

"Remember," he scolded, "it's strictly forbidden for a policeman to swear."

Vledder knew DeKok's opinion about strong language, but ignored the remark

"But ... but," he stammered with indignation, "Andrew never said anything about a son."

DeKok nodded listlessly.

"Indeed, and that puts Andrew right back in our rogue's gallery of possible suspects." He sighed elaborately, dramatically. "And as if one jolt wasn't enough, old man Kruger just told me that he found Drunnen's fingerprints all over the papers at villa *Jolanda*."

"But, why not?"

DeKok lowered his head into his hands in a weary gesture.

"Sure, but not on letters that by rights should not have been moved, or looked at, for the last thirty years, or more."

They remained silent after that remark. Vledder looked at his old mentor and suddenly realized what was needed.

"You know what we both need?" he said suddenly.

"What?"

"Cognac."

A happy smile lit up the craggy features of the old sleuth. He stood up with renewed vigor and placed a comradely arm around the shoulders of young Vledder. Gently he urged him forward.

"You're absolutely right ... Lowee's place can be very soothing."

* * *

The two Inspectors ambled slowly through the Quarter and at the corner of Barn Alley they sidled into Lowee's Place. They shoved the heavy, leather-bordered curtains aside and stepped into another world. Lowee's bar was one of those bars that are commonly referred to as "brown" bars. A lot of old-fashioned panelling, a wood floor and a ceiling that had never been painted. Presumably the "brown" came from the layers of nicotine that had adhered to the ceiling over the years. Most of the so-called "brown" bars had been functioning as drinking establishments for centuries. A "brown" bar is the Dutch equivalent of an English Pub. Some were historical monuments and it was not difficult to imagine 17th Century sailors sitting around the rough wooden tables, drinking beer and *jenever* and puffing on long, clay pipes.

It was cool, quiet and almost dark within Lowee's place. A young whore at one of the tables was flirting professionally with a middle-aged man. Three empty bottles littered the table and DeKok concluded idly that the young woman understood her profession. Black Ginny was sitting at the bar.

The small barkeeper looked up in surprise as Vledder and DeKok stepped up to the bar.

"Speak of the devil . . ." he said.

DeKok pointed a thumb at Vledder.

"The devil brought his colleague."

Lowee's mousy face contorted into a smile that expressed genuine pleasure at seeing DeKok.

"Ginny and me was just talking about you. She'd been reading them papers. She knows that geezer, she said, the brother, I mean."

"Jonathan?"

Little Lowee nodded and took a bottle from underneath the bar. With an easy slight-of-hand he placed three large snifters next to the bottle.

"You too, young gentleman?" he asked mockingly.

"Yes, please." answered Vledder. He was not offended. Lowee and DeKok liked each other, could almost be considered friends. But that was about as far as Lowee's tolerance of the police went. If Vledder had not been with DeKok, Lowee might have ignored him completely.

The barkeeper poured with a generous hand.

"I says to Ginny, I says . . . iffen you knows that guy, you gotta tell 'em. DeKok wants to know, I'm sure. Am I right, or am I right?"

He cocked an eye at DeKok who nodded. Black Ginny drifted closer.

"I know Jonathan," she said. Her tone of voice suggested that she already had a few drinks. "A dear, dear boy."

DeKok gave her a friendly smile.

"Would you like something to drink?" he asked politely.

"A martini."

DeKok motioned toward Lowee.

"A martini for the lady."

Her eyes lit up with pleasure.

"Our knight in shining armor," she chuckled. "The most gallant cop on the force." She laughed hoarsely. "Still chasing thieves and murderers?"

DeKok pulled a sad face.

"It's my fate," he confessed.

She hoisted herself on a barstool and leaned confidentially up against him.

"But this time you're wrong, old man. Completely wrong." She took a deep swallow of her drink. "Jonathan isn't the man you're after. You don't want him, take my word for it. Jonathan is . . . Jonathan is a gentleman," she concluded with quiet dignity.

DeKok took a sip from his cognac.

"I see," he said, "and a gentleman doesn't commit murder?"

She gave him a compassionate smile.

"Jonathan is too much of a gentleman to take care of something like that himself. You understand what I'm saying? If he wanted to get rid of his family, he'd *hire* somebody to do the job."

DeKok nodded to himself as if he had known it all along.

"How did you get to know him?"

She waved vaguely.

"You know, the usual, business."

DeKok looked at her with disbelief written all over his face. Black Ginny looked at him, correctly evaluated his expression and nonchalantly took a cigarette from an open pack on the bar.

"Does that surprise you?"

DeKok found some matches next to the cigarettes and hastened to light her cigarette.

"You're a beautiful woman, Ginny," he flattered.

She inhaled deeply, filling her lungs with smoke.

"Before . . . in my early days . . . then, yes, then I was beautiful." Smoke curled from her mouth. "Beautiful . . . and elegant." She slid from the stool and walked up and down in front of the bar, the left hand on a swaying hip and the right hand, holding and waving the cigarette in the air. On her way back, she stumbled, lost her balance and fell. DeKok hastened to help her but before he could reach her she was already back on her feet. Stumbling on her spiked heels she returned to the barstool.

DeKok took her by an elbow and helped her up.

"Stay with me," he ordered softly, "and tell me about Jonathan."

She rubbed a painful knee.

"Jonathan . . . Jonathan liked to throw parties." She cocked her head at him with a mischievous expression. "Parties in a house at St. John Street. Parties for friends. Sometimes they needed girls."

"And then he called you?"

She nodded complacently.

"Yes, he knew he could trust me to get the right kind of girls. I would go out and gather them up. Usually the same girls. The girls liked to go to Jonathan's parties. He paid extremely well."

"What sort of friends would be there?"

A sad look came into her eyes.

"The sort of friends a man like that usually has." It sounded solemn, melancholy. "Not real friends. Leeches, parasites with expensive suits." She sighed. "Sometimes I felt sorry for him."

"Did Jonathan really want to get rid of his family?"

She leaned over, found her glass and drained it.

"Ach, when Jonathan was drunk he'd say all sorts of things."

"Such as?"

She shook her head indulgently, smiled at the memory.

"A million for the one who rids me of that old hag."

"His mother?"

Black Ginny looked at him with a serious look in her glazed eyes.

"He hated her with a passion."

15

DeKok's phone rang. Somewhat bored, he moved to answer it.

"Well, how much longer is it going to take?" The voice sounded angry, agitated. DeKok recognized Margo Stover. "Tell that guy to go home," she continued.

"What guy?" he asked innocently.

"I can see him from my window in the portico across the street. It's a guy with an idiotic beret and a light-blue suit."

DeKok coughed.

"That guy, as you call him, is Detective-Sergeant Robert Antoine Dijk. A young and very fine policeman."

"Of course, a detective." The agitated tone in her voice persisted. "You told him to follow me."

"I was afraid," sighed DeKok, "that something might happen to you."

"I can take care of myself."

"In that case . . . I, . . . eh, I've been worrying for nothing."

A most un-feminine snorting sound came very clearly over the line.

"Worry . . . you don't worry about me. You just don't believe me, that's all. You thought I would lead you to Jonathan."

"That too."

"Well, I'm not going to Jonathan for the simple reason that I don't know where he is. So, you can just tell your Detective-Sergeant to take a hike."

"How long has he been standing there?"

"At least two hours, I guess."

DeKok hesitated.

"Margo . . . would you do something for me?"

"It depends . . ."

"Call him inside and ask him if he would like a cup of coffee."

"The *Inspector*?"

"Yes."

"I prefer to select my own company, thank you."

DeKok sighed a long-suffering sigh.

"All right, all right. Never mind. Just tell him from me that he can return to the station."

"I'm not being followed anymore?"

DeKok laughed.

"At least not by a man in a light-blue suit and a crazy beret . . . bye, bye . . . Margo."

He replaced the receiver and looked at Vledder.

"She made Dijk."

"That's what I gathered from the conversation."

"We better leave her alone for the time being. Now that she knows we are interested in her, she'll be twice as alert. But try to find out something more about her. Background and such. What exactly is her relationship with Jonathan? Is it really more than the usual flirtation? Call Town-Hall in Edam and see if there's anything about the intended nuptials."

Vledder looked at him with surprise.

"You think it's important?"

DeKok nodded pensively.

"Jonathan Weer is thirty-three. He doesn't need permission from parents, or guardians, to get married. It's just possible he kept it a secret from everybody."

Vledder shrugged his shoulders.

"So what?

DeKok did not answer but went over to the coffeepot and poured himself a mug of coffee. As usual, no milk, but loaded with sugar. Slowly he ambled back to his desk. He had decided to ignore Vledder's question with the sublime indifference that was able to bring some people to the verge of tears.

"You found out the location of the yacht?"

"Yes, *Julia* is moored in Horn. In the outer harbor. No crew."

"No crew?"

Vledder consulted his notes, anticipating the next questions.

"No, Jerome fired them all."

"When?"

"A few days ago." There was indignation in Vledder's voice. "They received a month's wages and a letter that stated that the yacht had been Henry's hobby and that he, Jerome wasn't planning to indulge himself that way. Ergo ... with thanks for past services ... get out of here."

"Rather harsh."

"People in Horn think it's scandalous."

"Has the yacht been sold?"

Vledder shook his head.

"No. It's an expensive ship. She won't be easy to sell."

"Is it part of the inheritance?"

"Oh, yes. *Julia* is the private property of the Weer family. According to my information, Henry and his wife were very much enamored of the yacht. They used her a lot. Personally, I think that Jerome must have planned to fire the crew for some time, but probably didn't dare to do so while the old lady was still alive."

DeKok nodded, slurped comfortably from his coffee and then looked at Vledder over the rim of his mug.

"Any news about the parents of the drowned sailor?"

Again Vledder consulted his notebook.

"*John Peter Opperman,*" he read, "*unmarried, son of Klaas Opperman and Neeltje Opperman, nee Rijpkema, residing at his parent's domicile at 27 Wester Street in Horn.*"

DeKok smiled.

"You always write it down like that?"

Vledder closed his notebook.

"The verbatim words of the clerk at the Registry," he said curtly. "And you should also know," he continued in a more conversational tone, "that John Peter Opperman is not officially dead yet."

DeKok placed his mug on the desk and looked up.

"The body hasn't been found," he concluded.

Vledder agreed.

"His parents still hope for a miracle," he said.

There was a long silence. Vledder doodled on the edge of the Police Gazette and DeKok, after giving his coffee another stir with a letter opener, slowly slurped it down. When he had emptied the mug, he placed it carefully on a corner of the desk and resumed the conversation.

"We still have Juliette's purse and her clothes," he remarked. "They're in the evidence room. It's about time we return them. Why don't you call Andrew Bearburgh and ask him to stop by and pick them up?"

"You'll want a receipt?"

"Of course. Make a complete inventory and have him sign for everything. Then, ask him where Juliette bought the chinchilla coat."

"And if he doesn't know?"

"Ask him if, in the interest of the investigation, we may keep it a little longer. I've a feeling about that . . ."

The phone interrupted him. DeKok lifted the receiver and heard the Watch Commander at the other end of the line.

"There's a gentleman down here. He's asking for you."

DeKok smirked.

"A gentleman with slicked-down black hair, a turtle-neck sweater and suede shoes?"

"The Watch Commander hesitated for a moment.

"I can't see the shoes from where I'm sitting, but the rest is as advertised."

"Excellent, really excellent. Send him up."

* * *

Jan (Johannes) Marie Antoine Drunnen *did* wear suede shoes. He crossed the detective room with quick, resolute steps. Reddened spots on his cheeks provided some color to his pale face.

"When is this nonsense going to stop?" he called from halfway across the room "I can't just drop everything I'm doing to come to the police station whenever you feel like talking to me. Arrest the murderer and leave me alone!"

DeKok bowed formally.

"Good evening, Mr. Drunnen," he said calmly and with a friendly smile. "Please have a seat."

"Thank you."

"And then, please, tell me *which* murderer you would like me to arrest."

Drunnen looked as if he could not believe his ears.

"Jonathan Weer, who else? I read in the papers this morning that there's not a shadow of a doubt about that."

DeKok pursed his lips and nodded to himself.

"And . . . *which* murder?"

Drunnen moved restlessly in his chair.

"Which murder . . . which murder? *Both* murders, of course. That seems pretty obvious to me."

"And the motive?"

Drunnen swallowed.

"Hey, wait a moment," he said impatiently. "Who's in charge of the investigation? I'm no cop."

DeKok looked at him with guileless astonishment.

"But it was obvious to you, you said."

Drunnen laughed nervously.

"I . . . I, well, that's to say, I go by what is printed in the papers."

DeKok grinned. It was not his usual, boyish grin. But an unpleasant version of that. It made Drunnen more uncomfortable and he ran his tongue along dry lips.

"Remarkable," observed DeKok after letting his opponent squirm for a while. "Isn't it remarkable? You rely on what's printed in the papers, while you *know* that what's written in the papers is wrong."

Drunnen squirmed some more.

"I know the papers are wrong?" he asked suspiciously.

DeKok nodded emphatically.

"Most certainly," he said sharply. "You're very much aware that at least *one* of the murders could never have been committed by Jonathan." He leaned closer to Drunnen. "And you know that, Mr. Drunnen, for the simple reason that *you*, nobody else, but you killed Mrs. Weer-Brockenheim, the widow of Henry Weer."

Drunnen jumped up, wildly gesticulating.

"It's a lie . . . all lies. I didn't do it! It isn't true! I didn't kill her." He raised his right hand. "As God is my witness," he declared.

DeKok looked at him with a poker face.

"An important witness," he said evenly. "An important witness indeed, but we cannot subpoena Him."

Drunnen looked at him, confusion and fear battled for supremacy.

"You *must* believe me."

"Why?" was the sobering question.

Drunnen swallowed again. The expressionless, merciless attitude of the old sleuth confused him, destroyed the last vestiges of his equilibrium. He leaned over the desk and gripped DeKok by the lapels of his jacket.

"I didn't do it! I DIDN'T DO IT!!" He screamed it out in a wild, uncontrolled voice that broke under the stress. "You can't accuse me like that! YOU CAN'T DO THAT! I was never there!"

DeKok could feel the young man's hot breath on his face. With a casual gesture that belied enormous strength, he gripped Drunnen's wrists and pressed him back in the chair across the desk. In the same expressionless, cold voice DeKok added more information.

"We have your fingerprints."

Drunnen looked at him with wide eyes. His mouth fell open.

"That's impossible," he managed eventually. "That's impossible. I went through the office . . ." He stopped suddenly. Naked, animal fear showed in his eyes.

DeKok nodded slowly.

" . . . and wiped everything clean," he completed. "I know. But you forgot that fingerprints can also be retained by paper."

It took several seconds before DeKok's words penetrated. When he realized what had been said, Drunnen hid his face in his hands and started to cry.

"She was dead already . . . she was dead already . . . she was dead already," he repeated over and over in a monotonous litany.

16

DeKok rose from behind his desk and walked away from Jan Drunnen. The seemingly weak young man did not strike a sympathetic chord with him, he did not like him. It was pure prejudice, he knew, and for that he was angry with himself. In DeKok's old-fashioned code of ethics there were times when men were permitted to cry, but never, he felt, because they were simply sorry for themselves. He paced up and down the large detective room with an irate look on his face, dodging the many obstacles with subconscious ease and totally shutting out the background noise in the busy room.

He asked himself if Jan Drunnen was capable of murder. Physically there was no doubt. He had an opportunity to measure the strength of the young man when he, with such apparent ease, had freed himself from Drunnen. But psychologically? Did he have the moral courage, the inclination to strangle an old woman, or knock her down? It was a moot point and DeKok was well aware of it. He had seen scores of murderers during his long career. They had ranged from cool professionals with strong, sinewy hands to nervous shooters who were barely able to keep their weapon steady.

What made a person a murderer was never predictable. In his early days, his salad days, he had often tried to approach the concept from a sober, intellectual point of view. He had tried to be objective. But the older he became, the more he was inclined to ignore the intellectual, cool, objective views in the matter. He found himself reacting more and more to his instinct, his feelings. His opinions, his thought processes seemed to become more subjective. Feelings . . . in his early days he had laughed at them, suppressed them as unreliable, irrational, impossible to take into account.

DeKok finally halted behind Drunnen who was now leaning on the desk, his head hidden inside his folded arms, his shoulders heaving in the grip of sorrow and self-pity.

"She was dead already . . . she was dead already . . ."

He kept repeating it, over and over.

DeKok stretched out an arm and tapped him on the shoulder.

"Sit up straight," he ordered, but his tone was gentle. As Drunnen complied, DeKok moved again behind his desk, sat down and looked at the tear-stained face in front of him.

"Where did you find her?"

Drunnen sighed a deep, shuddering sigh.

"In her bedroom, upstairs."

"On the floor?"

"No . . . no, she was on the bed."

"How?"

"On her back, dressed . . . with, with her eyes open."

"How did you know she was dead?"

A tic developed on Drunnen's face that threatened to distort his features.

"I . . . I talked to her. I called her name. Mrs. Weer, I said. Softly at first, but . . . but then louder. Then . . . I took her by the hand." Again he burst out in tears and cried loudly, with long, loud wails. A few of the detectives in the room looked up and some of the "regular" customers of the detective branch, being interviewed at various desks, looked upon him with disgust. "She was dead already," he repeated again. "I didn't do it. Believe me, it was the burglar." The words were punctuated by the sound-effects of his weeping.

DeKok's eyebrows vibrated briefly.

"Burglar?"

"Somebody had broken in."

"Where?"

"Downstairs, in the small office. I climbed in through the broken window. There was a lot of glass on the gravel outside. Lots of glass. The entire window had been knocked out of the frame. I didn't know what had happened, I didn't understand. I thought . . ." He had started to talk faster, more staccato. DeKok raised a hand to stem the flow of words.

"Calm, Drunnen, calm down. Tell me everything exactly as it happened. Don't start in the middle. Why were you at the villa?"

"Mrs. Weer had summoned me."

"How?"

"She called me on the phone at about one-thirty, shortly after lunch, and asked me to come over."

"Why?"

"I don't know. She wanted to discuss something, she said."

"Were you supposed to bring something? Papers, documents, business papers?"

Drunnen shook his head.

"She didn't say anything about that. It was a short, barking call, as we were used to get from her . . . *be here at three*, she said."

"Did you discuss this with anybody?"

"My secretary. She had to cancel some appointments."

DeKok nodded understanding.

"You went by car?"

"Yes, my own car. If the traffic is light it's only twenty minutes from the office to the villa. I had plenty of time. maybe I was a few minutes early. I parked the car in front of the house and rang the doorbell. I waited for a while, but nobody opened the door. I thought it a bit strange because the old lady was always very punctual. Usually she would wait behind the door and would open it as soon as you arrived. I looked at my watch, I remember doing that, and it was already past three. I rang the bell again . . . and again." Drunnen gripped his head with both hands. "I should have just left, then. Nothing would have happened. You wouldn't have found my fingerprints and . . ."

"But you didn't leave?" interrupted DeKok.

Jan Drunnen shook his head, wiping his eyes.

"I was worried. I really was, believe me. Not that I liked her very much . . . nobody really liked her, but after all, she was an old lady. So, I walked around the house, thinking she might be in the garden, in the back. She spent a lot of time there. She loved her garden. But I saw nobody. I checked the garden gate, but it was locked. So, I walked back around the other side of the house."

"That's when you saw the glass?"

"Yes, I stepped on it."

"Then what?"

"I looked to see where the glass had come from, of course, and discovered the busted window. Most of the glass had already been removed from the frame, so I carefully climbed in. I saw at once that somebody had searched the office and I assumed it was the work of a burglar. I waited and listened carefully. You see, at that moment I figured that the burglar might still be in the house. But I heard nothing, everything was quiet. So, I went further into the house, but I still couldn't hear anything. No suspicious sounds, or anything. After I had searched the rooms downstairs, I went upstairs."

"And you found her?"

"Dead." Drunnen fell silent and bowed his head.

DeKok coughed.

"Go on," he said sharply, "this isn't the end of your story."

Drunnen looked at him and slowly shook his head, a look of despair in his eyes.

"No," he answered in a rasping voice. "That's not the end." He scratched his forehead, "I should have called the police when I found her."

"Why didn't you?"

Drunnen rubbed the back of his hand along dry lips. The nervous tics reappeared on his face and he blinked his eyes several times.

"Why didn't you?" repeated DeKok.

"It's a long story."

"I'm listening."

Drunnen swallowed.

"I owe a lot to old Henry," he began. "Let me say that first of all. I can never think ill of the man. On the contrary, without him I would probably never be much more than just one more bookkeeper with talent . . . but a low salary." He sighed. "And maybe not even that."

"Go on," urged DeKok.

A wan, tired smile fled across Drunnen's face.

"It's now almost ten years ago. I was twenty-three, four at the time. I was employed in an administrative capacity at CIH, nothing special. But I did work hard in order to get ahead. I took night classes, studying for my CPA. I also studied languages."

He closed his eyes, reflecting, then he went on.

"One day I met Nanette. I was stunned, she took my breath away . . . I was in love at first sight, in love as I had not thought possible. She made me walk on clouds, just by looking at me. She was extremely beautiful, exquisite with a strong sexual desire and . . ." He laughed cynically. ". . . and a long list of other desires and wishes." He shrugged his shoulders. "I didn't care. I would have done anything for her. I would have robbed the Bank of Holland and the bank of England both, had she told me to do it. I somehow existed from one meeting to the next. I only felt alive when I was with her and I neglected everything . . . Didn't care about anything else . . . work, classes, everything. And when the money was gone . . . I stole."

Again he paused, rubbed his teary eyes with a weary hand.

"You see, I had discovered a loophole in the administrative system of CIH. Although I never laid my hands on any actual cash, I was not in charge of that, I was able to divert the equivalent of almost fifty thousand dollars to my own pockets in the period of a few months. I thought I had it made, but I also knew the bubble would burst sooner or later."

"And it did?"

Drunnen looked into the distance, ignoring the question.

"One day," he continued, "old Henry told me to come to his office."

"And?"

"I fully expected to find a cop waiting for me. I had already prepared myself for that eventuality. But old Henry was alone. He offered me a chair and told me straight-out that he had discovered my fraud, the embezzlement. He said that he admired my ingenuity and asked me all sorts of questions . . . How I had done it and why. When I had told him everything, he placed a written confession in front of me wherein it stated that I had been guilty of embezzling large sums of money from CIH. He ordered me to sign it and I did."

"What about paying back the money?"

Drunnen shook his head.

"He never mentioned the money. Not a word. He picked up the phone and summoned all managers and department heads to his office. When they were all gathered together, he announced me as Deputy General Manager and Chief Administrative Officer."

"What!?" DeKok was stunned and showed it.

Drunnen nodded his head slowly, with emphasis.

"Yes, young as I was . . . Assistant General Manager and Chief Administrative Officer. Nobody understood it. Me, least of all. The only conditions he set were that I break my relationship with Nanette and continue my studies. That was all. The confession he kept as a sort of certificate with which he bought my loyalty."

DeKok looked at him searchingly.

"A certificate to buy your loyalty?"

"Yes, that's what he called it. All these years it has been hanging over my head. I was his spiritual prisoner. Although he never said another word about it, I felt the threat of exposure in every sentence he uttered. It made me a slave. In a very literal sense he *owned* me."

He shook his head, raked his fingers through his hair and sighed deeply.

"Later, much later, I understood that my sudden promotion had been more than a whim. Because of my new position I was obliged to closely monitor all monetary transactions. Old Henry and his wife were firm believers in the old adage that 'it takes a thief to catch a thief' and I was the thief that was supposed to watch out for them."

DeKok smiled.

"A remarkable couple."

Drunnen looked at him with weary, resigned eyes.

"A remarkable family. Cunning, malevolent, with an almost devilish ability to bind people to them, control them. Me . . . I found being a slave to one person more than enough."

DeKok's eyes narrowed.

"The confession?"

Drunnen nodded.

"Exactly. After Henry died I looked everywhere for that damned document. I practically ransacked his office and went through all his papers. But I couldn't find it. There was only one place left to look, only one other place where it could be."

"The private office at the villa," remarked DeKok.

Vledder sighed elaborately, but kept quiet.

"It was an unique chance. You must see that. Ten years is a long time to live with a constant threat. Never knowing when the scandal would break, when I would be exposed. When I found old lady Weer dead, I immediately realized that the only two people who knew about my . . . my indiscretion, were now dead. Nobody else knew. If I left it at the villa then, sooner or later, either Jerome, or Jonathan, would inevitably find it. I would be right back where I started, slave to a different master."

DeKok looked long and hard at Drunnen. His initial prejudice had subsided. He now understood the tension under which the young man had lived most of his life.

"Did you find it?"

Drunnen lowered his head.

"In between some old letters. My hands shook when I finally had the paper in my possession. After that I wiped the desk and everything else in the office I might have touched. Then I climbed out through the broken window. I was half-drunk with happiness as I drove back to the city. I stopped near the river and tore it up in a thousand pieces and let it blow away on the wind. The last I saw of it were small pieces of paper on the water. A sea-gull was chasing a few pieces." He smiled at the memory. "It was one of the most beautiful sights of my life."

DeKok nodded vaguely, did not ask anything else. Drunnen's explanation seemed reasonable. But he realized that it was a single, one-sided story, unconfirmed by any third party. It *could* have been that way. It did answer a lot of questions, but . . . left the most important question unanswered. Who killed the old lady?

DeKok scratched the back of his neck while he studied Drunnen. Again he noted the somewhat insipid mouth, the brown, moist eyes. Could he have been capable of committing both murders, or one of them? The thought haunted him.

"Did you love Juliette?"

An alert, suspicious look came into Drunnen's eyes.

"We . . . we met each other."

DeKok shook his head.

"I knew that and it isn't what I asked. I asked if you loved her?"

Drunnen sighed.

"Juliette was an extremely beautiful woman, frivolous, humorous and with an amazing temperament."

DeKok listened carefully to the tone of voice.

"You didn't love her," he concluded out loud.

Drunnen did not react at once. He studied the nails of his right hand, avoided DeKok's eyes.

"If you value the word *love*," he vacillated finally, "it wasn't *real* love."

DeKok nodded understanding.

"How did you arrange your meetings?"

"I wrote her a note."

"And you had that delivered?"

"One of the office boys used to pass her house on the way home. He would drop it in the mail slot for me."

"237 Mirrors Canal?"

"Yes, that's where she lived."

DeKok opened a drawer and took from it the envelope he had found in Juliette's purse. He held it up, the address side toward Jan Drunnen.

"You recognize this?"

Drunnen seemed astonished.

"That's my envelope . . . my handwriting."

DeKok's face hardened. He turned the envelope around and pointed at the name of the sender.

"Jonathan, it says here."

17

Vledder did not understand it. He spread his arms wide, palms out, in a display of vexation and incomprehension.

"You let him go," he exclaimed, baffled. "You just let him walk right out of the station! Why? We have more than reasonable ground . . . It wasn't Jonathan who wrote the letter, but Drunnen. Jonathan didn't have an appointment with Juliette, but Drunnen did and it wasn't Jonathan who placed Juliette in Slate Makers Alley . . ."

A broad grin appeared on DeKok's face.

". . . but Jan Drunnen."

Vledder looked at him in surprise.

"Well, what's so strange about that?"

DeKok shook his head.

"There's nothing strange about that. But it's a precipitous conclusion, solely based on the fact that Jan Drunnen signed his letters to Juliette with Jonathan's name. We can't ask Juliette anymore, but it's not at all improbable that it happened at *her* request. We do know how jealous Andrew was, and is. He kept pursuing her, even after the divorce." He winked at Vledder. "So, you see, when Juliette received a letter from her brother, there was no reason for Andrew to be jealous. If Jan Drunnen had signed the letters with his own name, Andrew would have immediately been suspicious, followed by accusations, scenes, quarrels. Neither Juliette, nor Drunnen, were interested in that."

"A red herring!"

DeKok nodded agreement.

"A game . . . a childish prank to mislead Andrew. And it worked."

"How's that?"

DeKok raised one finger in an admonishing gesture.

"When you asked Bearburgh if he knew anything about a lover of his ex-wife who fitted the description you gave him, Andrew didn't, at first, know whom you were talking about. When he finally made the connection between the description and Jan Drunnen, he was both amazed and angry. He had not known it before. It was a complete surprise to him. Yet, thanks to Red Tina, we know that the relationship must have lasted some time."

Vledder sank back in his chair.

"You're right," he sighed bitterly. "But the question remains: *who* had an appointment with Juliette on the night of her death? Drunnen, Jonathan . . . or a third person?"

DeKok moved to the window and leaned against the window-sill.

"We now know," he lectured, "that the envelope in Juliette's purse is no real clue, at least, not a clue that points to Jonathan. At first glance, again in the light of what we know, it might be a clue that points in the direction of Drunnen. But . . . Kruger tells us that it's an old envelope. It's also possible that the envelope doesn't play a part in this at all, at all. Juliette could have carried it around for sentimental reasons. Drunnen confirms it's an old envelope. According to him, his last meeting with her was exactly ten days before her death. He denies vehemently having had a date with her on the night in question. Of course, to be on the safe side, we'll ask the office boy when he last delivered a letter to the Mirrors Canal, but I'm almost sure it will check out."

Vledder nodded resignedly.

"Jonathan, after all." It sounded like a curse.

DeKok shrugged his shoulders.

"Remember the medallion . . . the antique dealer . . . the passport. Jonathan is still the man we're looking for."

"Strange, though, that he's managed to remain so elusive."

DeKok pursed his lips.

"Yes," he agreed, "he seems to have a knack for disappearing without a trace. Any news from Interpol?"

Vledder laughed without mirth.

"Just a short message."

"Oh, yes?"

Vledder rummaged in a drawer and unearthed a pink telex message.

"It states that Weer, Jonathan, appears just once on the blotters of the Paris police regarding the unauthorized possession of seventy ampules of morphine."

"What!?"

"Seventy ampules of morphine."

"You could have told me that sooner." It sounded like a reprimand.

Vledder looked crest-fallen.

"But it isn't recent," he apologized. "It happened almost two years ago. Of course, I immediately followed up, but it was a storm in a teacup. During routine customs check at the Paris airport, the ampules were found in his suitcase. Apparently the customs people had been tipped off in advance. Jonathan stated that he knew nothing about it. He had no idea how the morphine wound up in his suitcase and suspected a bad practical joke from one of his friends."

"Was he arrested?"

"No, just fined."

DeKok placed a fatherly hand on Vledder's shoulder.

"You're right," he admitted. "It really isn't important. I wouldn't have the foggiest how to fit it in the overall picture."

He went back to his desk and sat down on it. He placed his hands on either side and dangled his legs in the air. Thoughtfully he stared at the floor.

"The case is really starting to bother me," he said after a while. "It's almost a week since we found Juliette's body and we haven't made any progress to speak of. It's too absurd, two murders and not a clue about a killer."

"*Three* murders and no killer," corrected Vledder.

DeKok grunted.

"Tomorrow," he announced, "I'm going to Horn. There's *got* to be a clue somewhere, some trace, some indication. No matter how careful the killer is . . . he *must* have made a mistake somewhere. They all do, sooner or later." He jumped off the desk. "And you, tomorrow, you go see Jerome and ask about old lady Weer's Last Will and Testament. Ask who's executor of the estate, if any. Find out about the lawyer." He looked thoughtfully at the clock on the wall, one hand leaning on the recently vacated desk. "Is Jerome married?" he asked.

Vledder answered while flipping through the pages of his notebook.

"Yes, he's been married for about ten years. A nice wife and two darling daughters."

"Aha, more grandchildren, after all."

"Yes."

"Any problems?"

Vledder smiled.

"No, no, pure old-fashioned solid Dutch respectability. They're very well known in Abcoude. Jerome is a member of several civic groups and young Mrs. Weer is very active in charitable organizations."

DeKok thoughtfully chewed his lower lip.

"I wonder," he mused, "if old Henry made any financial provisions for Drunnen. After all, he was considered Henry's protege . . . whatever the background of *that* may be. Also, let's not forget, Drunnen's first name also starts with a 'J' and Henry was a little touched on that subject." He walked over to the coat rack and took down his coat.

"Keep an eye on Drunnen," he said, throwing his coat over an arm. "Also, don't forget about Jerome . . . have another talk with Margo Stover and, above all, take care of yourself."

He placed his decrepit little felt hat on his head and walked out of the room.

Vledder had a surprised look on his face as he watched him leave.

* * *

Detective-Inspector DeKok entered the Central Railroad Station, bought a ticket to Horn and, breasting a stream of incoming commuters, worked his way toward Platform 13A, the local train to Horn.

He could have taken a car, but it was typical of DeKok to take the train. If Vledder was not there to do the driving, DeKok preferred to stay away from cars altogether. While indulging his well-known prejudices against all things modern, he soothed himself with the thought that, by taking the train, he was making his contribution to traffic safety. DeKok had no illusions about his driving skills.

He placed his hat on the overhead rack and snuggled comfortably into the corner of the window seat. Since nobody was seated across from him, he took off his heavy shoes and placed his feet tenderly on the opposite bench. His feet were tired. A battalion of little devils was poking red-hot needles into his calves. DeKok knew the symptoms and was grateful that Vledder could not observe him at this moment. This particular feeling in his legs only came when he was at a dead-end, was getting far from a solution. His legs played "hot" and "cold" with him in those circumstances. Some people could predict rain by the feeling in their corns, DeKok could tell how well he was progressing by the feeling in his legs. And, he admitted, his legs had seldom betrayed him.

The killer must feel reasonably safe. DeKok understood that. Jonathan was a cosmopolitan who was at home in most places. It would be easy for him to hide under a false name in Paris, Zurich, Barcelona, Istanbul, wherever. He would be lost in the crowd, become part of the landscape. He could keep that up until the uproar about the murders had subsided. Then, in the fullness of time, he could claim his part of the inheritance, if necessary through a lawyer, or some other third party. A hefty bundle of CIH shares would assure a comfortable living anywhere in the world.

The train creaked into motion, swayed across a series of switches, passed some warehouses and, gathering speed, headed north.

DeKok rubbed the bridge of his nose with a little finger. There was something wrong with his reasoning, it did not satisfy, it did not compute, as Vledder used to say. If Jonathan had wanted a quiet, comfortable life, the murders made no sense at all. Worse, they were superfluous, unnecessary. The Weers controlled an enormous capital and Jonathan's share was more than sufficient to guarantee him a life of leisure and luxury. DeKok shook his head. Jonathan wanted more. He wanted CIH and the power position that entailed. In that light the murders were . . .

Suddenly he discovered a young woman. She was seated to the left, across the aisle. He looked at her and studied her profile against the light reflected from towering cumulus clouds. A beautiful profile, he thought, fascinating, with a high forehead, a classical nose and long, glistening hair that spilled over her shoulders. Long legs emerged from a short skirt. She had crossed one leg over the other and the left leg rocked in cadence with the movement of the train. It was an extremely attractive left leg, with a smooth, round knee and a slender ankle. It forced its attention upon DeKok. The wagging leg fixated him, mesmerized him and his thoughts drifted away, far from the train and the cumulus clouds above the endless lowlands. Away to Margo, beautiful, blonde, exciting Margo. The train sped on. The monotonous cadence of the wheels penetrated his thoughts. Town-Hall-E-dam ... dum-dum-dum-dum ... Town-Hall-E-dam ... dum-dum-dum-dum ... Town-Hall-E-dam ... slowly DeKok fell asleep. He did not wake until Horn.

It was a bright, sunny day and Horn looked like a friendly, sleepy town. First the Dutch had closed off the former Zuyder Zee, then they had transformed more than two thirds of the area into land. Ecological concerns had spared the remaining one third and it had become the fresh-water Ijssel *Lake*, an important recreation area. A major seaport in the 17th Century, home to a large fishing fleet less than sixty years ago and now, with the closing of the enormous dike along the mouth of the inland sea and the completion of the incredible engineering feat that had made water into land, Horn was primarily a tourist attraction and a yachting harbor.

DeKok fished his hat from the overhead net, wriggled into his shoes and was the last to leave the train. The beauty with the exceptional legs walked about twenty yards in front of him. He noted with satisfaction that the right leg was no less shapely than the left. He smiled to himself. If he were to tell Vledder that he

181

had fallen asleep while looking at such legs, the younger man would most certainly advise him to take early retirement. He wondered what such an exotic beauty was doing in sleepy Horn. Without conscious volition he followed her.

He looked at his watch and saw that he had plenty of time. In any case, enough time to permit a little sidetracking in his investigation. She walked from the station to the small houses at the bottom of the dike. Apparently she was not sure where she was going, or what road to take. DeKok slowed down and allowed the distance between him and his quarry to increase. About halfway along the dike, she mounted a set of stairs. DeKok saw her accost an old man and ask for directions. The old man leaned forward and pointed further north.

DeKok hesitated a bit, then climbed the same stairs and followed her in the direction pointed out by the old man. To the right, below, was the yacht harbor filled with a veritable fleet of small, recreational sailboats. Flags hung limp at their posts. There was no wind. Gulls banished the silence with their screams.

The young woman walked in front of him on a cobble stone path across the grass. The path led to the *Dromedary*, the name of the old City Gate, actually the gate and the remains of an old fort. DeKok knew that a Student Center occupied the formidable old building and he suspected that it was the destination of his long-legged fellow passenger.

Much to his surprise, she passed through the gate toward an old cantilever bridge across a narrow canal. At the other side of the bridge she turned left. The ground sloped away from the high canal. Her step became firmer, more purposeful.

DeKok followed her tensely. He was now completely intrigued. Suddenly he saw her on the quay, near a beautiful yacht, sparkling white in the bright sunlight. Thanks to the convoluted street plan of the old town, DeKok had arrived at the outer harbor.

The woman stopped, hesitated, pushed the hair from her face. DeKok came closer. Over her shoulder he looked at the stern of the yacht and read the name aloud:

"*Julia*, Amsterdam."

18

She turned around and looked into DeKok's friendly face.

"It seems," she said in a surprised tone of voice, "that there's nobody aboard."

She spoke with a pleasant, lilting American accent.

DeKok shook is head slowly.

"There *is* nobody aboard," he said evenly. "The entire crew has been fired."

"Fired?" Her face reflected amazement and shock.

"And where is . . ."

". . . Jonathan Weer?"

A suspicious light gleamed in her eyes.

"You're the man from the train."

The gray sleuth bowed formally.

"Indeed, the sleeping man." He smiled. "allow me to introduce myself. My name is DeKok, DeKok with kay-oh-kay. I'm a police inspector from Amsterdam. And who are you?"

She pointed at the gleaming yacht.

"You're sure there's nobody aboard?"

DeKok waved nonchalantly.

"Shall we have a look?"

She hesitated. Then she led the way to the yacht. DeKo took her by the arm.

185

"On one condition," he said.

"Yes?"

"If there's nobody aboard, you'll allow me to buy you a cup of coffee."

A smile enriched her full lips.

"OK, policeman."

* * *

They were seated across from each other in the *Old Pepperhouse*, a former warehouse for East-Indian spices, now converted to a restaurant. Earlier DeKok had led her through the Zuyder Zee Museum but had not mentioned a word about the reason for her presence in Horn. It had become a game to see how tense, how nervous she would be.

He took a sip from his coffee and looked at her intently. Close by she lost none of her attractiveness. She looked at him, looking at her and tossed her head.

"I do believe I owe you some answers."

"If you'd rather not . . ."

She shook her head, creating a momentary cloud of gold-blonde hair.

"Why? I've nothing to hide. My name is Lucienne Dammen and I'm looking for Jonathan.

"Me too."

She stirred her coffee.

"I know. I read the papers. But Jonathan has nothing to do with the murders."

DeKok did not respond directly.

"You've known him long?"

"Yes," she nodded, "I've known him for some time, since I was sixteen. My parents were friends of the Weers before we emigrated to the States. But Jonathan and I stayed in touch.

Sometimes he would come to New York and sometimes I would come here during my vacations."

"On the yacht?"

"Those were beautiful weeks," she reminisced. "*Julia* is a splendid ship."

"When did you arrive?"

"Exactly one week ago. On the night Juliette was killed. I read it in the papers the next morning. Naturally, I was a bit hesitant to contact the family, under the circumstances. Old lady Weer didn't like me at all and I was never close to Jerome."

"Why did you come?"

"I received a letter from Jonathan." She reached for her purse. "I don't mind you reading it."

"Just tell me about it."

"He wrote that he had fallen in love with Margo and was planning to marry her."

DeKok studied her face.

"You were disappointed," he observed.

She blushed.

"I understood his position. He wanted the child to have his name."

DeKok's eyes widened slightly.

"Child?" he asked, amazement in his voice.

She played with the spoon in her hand.

"She was pregnant."

"Margo?"

"That's what Jonathan wrote to me." Her attitude changed suddenly, her voice became less dreamy, became sharper. "Jonathan doesn't fit in these times," she said with conviction. "He should have been born a few centuries ago. He's more the chivalrous type, a knight, a Galahad, a Lancelot, a . . ."

". . . Don Quixote?"

She lowered her head.

187

"Perhaps, yes," she said, calmer. "You see, Margo didn't have to be pregnant at all. Her saying so would be enough for Jonathan. He's very honest, trusting. It wouldn't occur to him that the slut might be lying."

DeKok nodded, more to himself than in agreement.

"And what about the murders?"

She shrugged her shoulders.

"Maybe they tried to prevent him getting married. That's happened before."

DeKok discerned a certain tone in her voice.

"You?"

She smiled sadly.

"Last year. Jonathan and I were about to be married."

"Who stopped it?"

"His mother. She ruled everybody and everything with an iron fist. Have you ever met her? With her hooked nose and small, piggy eyes. Eyes that saw everything, knew everything. Eyes that saw right through you. Just like a witch. They were all afraid of her . . . Jonathan, Jerome, Juliette . . . all of them."

DeKok drained the last of his coffee.

"Is Jonathan a morphine addict?" he asked tonelessly.

She looked at him with genuine astonishment.

"Whatever made you say that?"

"About eighteen, twenty months ago he was arrested at the Paris airport. He had seventy ampules of morphine in his luggage."

She laughed out loud.

"Those were not for Jonathan."

"Oh, for whom, then?"

"His father . . . his father was an addict."

* * *

188

He took her back to the train.

"Go back to New York, Lucienne."

"If Jonathan is in trouble," she said with determination, "I want to stand by him."

"There's nothing you can do for him." He held her hand and looked into her eyes. "Jonathan" he sighed, "is a lucky man."

"With you on his trail?" It sounded resentful.

He shook his head.

"No, no . . . because he has you for a friend."

"That's exactly the sort of thing," she responded softly, "that Jonathan would say."

DeKok made a dejected, almost helpless gesture.

"Sometimes," he said simply, "I'm a little bit of a knight myself."

With a sudden, impulsive gesture she planted a kiss on his forehead and climbed into the train.

When the train left the station he waved after her for a long time.

* * *

DeKok looked around. The room was small and painstakingly clean. A large photograph of a young man had pride of place on the mantel piece. It showed a pleasant, open face and a laughing mouth.

"Johan?"

The other man nodded. He was gray, almost white with a tanned face and clear, alert eyes.

"He was twenty-two at the time. It's the last photo we have of him."

"He's not been found yet?"

The old man growled.

"Johan has a seaman's grave. A seaman's grave is an honest grave."

DeKok did not argue the point.

"His interview in the paper did cause quite a stir at the time."

"Yes?"

"Wouldn't it have been better if Johan had gone straight to the police with his suspicions?"

Johan's father grimaced.

"The Weers are powerful people with a lot of influence and powerful friends."

DeKok looked again at the picture.

"Johan didn't trust the police?"

The old man shook his head.

"You're trying to make me say things I don't want to say. The police are trustworthy enough. That wasn't the reason."

"What *was* the reason?"

"Publicity. We talked about it for a long time, Johan and I, and we wondered how we could get the necessary publicity. We didn't want it swept under the rug."

"Therefore, the press."

The old man nodded vehemently.

"Yes, indeedy, that was the answer. *Everybody* would know what had happened aboard. No way to hide it, then."

DeKok smiled.

"That's to say, as far as Johan knew, surely?"

The old man reacted sharply.

"My son was convinced that old Henry Weer had been murdered."

"And what convinced him?"

The old man's face became an obstinate mask. He moved uneasily in his chair, leaned forward.

"Conviction, truth and facts are different things, Mr. DeKok. I'm well aware of that. But just because our sort of people don't always know all the facts, the truth, we have to believe in our convictions. And that's a good thing . . . although you probably think differently. Johan was *convinced* that old Henry had been killed by his family and he *acted* on that conviction."

DeKok nodded calmly, a serious look in his eyes.

"But what are the facts?" he asked, emphasizing the last word in a cool tone of voice.

The elder Opperman sighed resignedly.

"Johan was an able seaman, an A/B, but he also acted as steward. That's not unusual on board those yachts. Johan had a good berth, no question about that. Old man Weer liked him and it was mutual. Henry Weer was a *humane* human being, if you know what I mean. But he had been ill for some time, suffered from gall stones. When he had an attack, or expected one, he took an injection. That's what the old witch did. She administered the shots."

"Mrs. Weer?"

"Yes, she was real handy with a needle. According to Johan she had been a nurse, in her younger days." The old man shrugged his shoulders. "We've all been things in our younger days," he said. He paused a moment, as if gathering his thoughts. Then he continued: "On the night in question old Henry rang from his cabin and my son responded immediately. It gave Johan quite a shock. When he entered the cabin he found the old man on the carpet, on his back, in a frenzy, sweating, with wild, scared eyes. Johan had never seen anything like it. The old man was writhing with pain and kept trying to hug his stomach. Johan knelt down, next to him, trying to help him. That's when Henry told him: *Get my wife, I've been poisoned.* and that's why Johan was convinced."

DeKok rubbed his face with a flat hand.

"And then Johan went to get old lady Weer?"

The other nodded.

"Yes. She came at once and had the hypodermic ready."

"Did she give him a shot?"

"I think so. But my son didn't know for sure. She sent him from the cabin." The old man started to stuff an old pipe with shaking hands. "Johan didn't want to leave, he wanted to stay with the old man. You see, he just *felt* there was something wrong, that something wasn't right."

"And?"

Tears sprang in Opperman's eyes.

"She chased him away like a dog," his voice quivered. "And half an hour later old Henry was dead." He wiped his eyes with the back of his hand and grimaced.

"Dr. Gelder stated that Henry had died a natural death."

The old man tamped the tobacco down in his pipe.

"That old witch could make anybody say anything she wanted them to say. Believe you me, they poisoned Henry Weer."

"But why?"

Opperman looked up at him in surprise. The tears had gone, the hands no longer shook. There was a fighting spirit in his eyes.

"It's your task to find out. I have told you what my son saw, heard and experienced. You must draw your own conclusions from that." He reached out and picked up a book a matches, prepared to put the flame to the bowl of his pipe." I can tell you something else," he continued, striking a match. "The day after it happened, a Mr. Drunnen came to the house and asked to speak to my son." He puffed a glow into the tobacco and extinguished the match. "Well, my boy was at work in the garden, in the back. So I let him through. And what do you think happened? That fine gentleman offered my boy five thousand guilders if he would keep his mouth shut."

"What!?"

Opperman nodded complacently, puffing on his pipe.

"Five thousand guilders," he repeated.

"Then what?"

The old man took the pipe from his mouth.

"We grabbed him and together we threw him out the door." He paused, a satisfied look on his face. Then a shadow fell over his face, he placed his pipe in an ashtray. "Two days later," he added in sober tones, "my son fell overboard and drowned."

"Any suspicions?"

The old man shook his head.

"No, there was no Weer on board," he said. "And the crew consisted of honest seamen."

19

Inspector DeKok left the large hall of the Central Railroad Station. It was well past nine o'clock and it was getting dark. He waited patiently for the pedestrian light to turn to green and then walked, past the streetcars, to the bridge. The blacktop on the huge Dam Square reflected the neon lights from the beer signs and bars. I should go home, he thought, where my wife is waiting patiently. But something drove him, an undefined feeling, an indescribable urge. It forced him to make his way to Warmoes Street. To the station house.

He hoisted himself up the stairs and found both Vledder and Dijk still in the large detective room. They were just about the only occupants at that time. He was not surprised to find them there. Somehow, he had expected it. The faces of the two young Inspectors looked serious, but their expressions changed when they saw him enter.

Vledder approached him, happily surprised.

"Have you been home yet?"

"No, I came straight from the train."

"Oh. I called your wife, earlier, and asked her to ask you to come back here."

DeKok cocked a weary eye at his young colleague.

"Something the matter?"

Vledder's face fell.

"This afternoon, there was an attempt on the life of little Andrew."

DeKok looked blank.

"Who's little Andrew?"

"The son of Andrew Bearburgh. The boy's in a boarding school in the south, in Eindhoven."

DeKok looked angry.

"How do you know it was attempted murder?"

"It came over the wire, less than an hour ago," explained Vledder. "With a request."

"What sort of request?"

"To arrest Andrew Bearburgh."

"What!?"

Vledder nodded seriously.

"Apparently he tried to run over his son with a car."

DeKok looked disgusted.

"You're seriously trying to tell me that Andrew Bearburgh tried to kill his own son?"

"Yes."

"Nonsense!"

Vledder looked at him, shook his head slowly.

"The boy says so himself."

DeKok sat down at his desk and hid his face in his hands. Suddenly he felt tired, weary, exhausted. His head felt empty, incapable of forming coherent thoughts. His body felt listless, as if all muscles had atrophied.

Vledder sat down across from him. His face was pale.

"What should we do?"

DeKok sighed deeply. With an extreme effort he overcame his temporary weakness.

"How's the boy?"

"As well as can be expected, considering the circumstances. A few bumps and bruises, a broken leg, but otherwise unhurt. The car just gave him a glancing blow and he fell to the side, on grass, and rolled away. It was his salvation."

"Where is he now?"

"In Eindhoven. In the sick-bay of the boarding school. The leg has been set. Happily there were no complications. But the boy was in shock."

"Small wonder. And he definitely identified his father?"

Vledder nodded reluctantly.

"Yes, no question. I checked back by telephone and I talked to the sergeant of the State Police. The boy was positive about that, he said."

DeKok stared into the distance and remained silent for several minutes.

"We're going to Eindhoven," he said suddenly.

Vledder looked confused.

"Now?"

"Yes, at once." DeKok sprang up from his chair and pointed at Dijk. "You're going to pick up Bearburgh. Go to his house. If he's home, bring him in."

"Arrest?"

DeKok shook his head, walking to the door.

"Ask him if he wants to come voluntarily," he tossed over his shoulder. "Ask for his cooperation. Don't tell him what happened. Just tell him it's in connection with Juliette's murder."

"If he doesn't want to come voluntarily?" called Dijk.

DeKok stopped his progress, turned around and walked back toward Dijk.

"Then you arrest him for murder," he said. He placed a hand on Dijk's shoulder. "But try to avoid it, you understand. I prefer to avoid a formal arrest. I'd like to keep it clean."

* * *

Vledder whipped the old police VW along the E9 toward the south. The speedometer seemed locked on sixty-five miles per hour, about all the tired old car was able to sustain, although the gas pedal was floored and Vledder kept it there. The car was meant for city patrol in the narrow streets and alleys of Amsterdam and was never meant to compete on the highways.

DeKok slumped in the seat and did not interfere with Vledder's driving, nor did he urge him to greater speed. He hoped to be in Eindhoven before midnight and he hoped to convince the management of the boarding school to let him talk to Bearburgh's son. He trusted Vledder to do whatever he could to get him there as soon as possible. He did not know why, but he felt it was important to hear the accusation from the boy's own mouth.

After a while DeKok glanced at Vledder, who did not take his eyes of the road, and made himself heard over the noise of the slip-stream and the rattling of the old car.

"Why was Dijk still in the office?"

"Because of the fur coat."

"What's the matter with it?"

"Andrew Bearburgh has never seen it before."

"He's been at the station once already." It was not a question, but a statement. Vledder responded, nevertheless.

"Yes, at about ten o'clock this morning. As we agreed, I called him to come and get Juliette's personal belongings. He was pretty nervous, he had tears in his eyes when he saw her stuff."

"The fur coat." prodded DeKok.

"He ignored it. Didn't recognize it. When I placed it on the table with the other stuff, her clothes and so, he pushed it aside. *That's not hers*, he said. I asked him if he was sure, but he said he

198

had never seen it before." He paused and concentrated on passing a tractor-trailer combination. "Also," he continued, when the obstacle had been passed and he was again in the right lane, "according to Andrew she wasn't wearing the coat that night while they were having dinner."

DeKok grinned suddenly.

"Of course not."

Taken aback, Vledder released the pressure on the gas pedal, slowed down and looked aside.

"You knew that?"

DeKok waved in the direction of the windshield.

"Keep going," he ordered, "we're late enough as it is."

Vledder again floored the pedal, but did not abandon the subject.

"You knew it all along," he accused.

DeKok scratched the back of his neck and tried to find some release for his cramped muscles.

"What sort of fashionable woman ... and Juliette *was* extremely fashionable ... wears a fur coat on a balmy summer night?"

"Well, she wore it when we found her."

"Yes. Our careful killer made a mistake, there."

"How's that."

"A weak moment. An act of piety toward the dead. The killer didn't want to dump his victim on the bricks just like that. She was cold, the bricks were cold and he wanted to take care of her, keep her warm. That's why he put the fur coat on her, you see. To keep her warm, to cover her."

"That would indicate some emotional connection."

DeKok sighed, but the sound was lost in the noise of their passing.

"An emotional connection," he repeated slowly, "a relationship of some kind. Yes, indeed. But it doesn't help us one little bit. That's why I didn't mention it before. All suspects had some sort of emotional connection with Juliette . . . Jan Drunnen, Andrew Bearburgh, Jonathan Weer . . . You can expect *some* gesture of piety toward Juliette from all of them."

Vledder kept his eyes glued to the road.

"I asked Dijk to find out where the coat came from. He came back tonight, dog-tired. He carried it from one furrier to the next."

"So, that's why he was still there. And?"

"Nothing."

DeKok grinned again.

"Have him check it out with Margo, tomorrow."

Vledder's face cleared for just a moment, banishing the look of concentration.

"That's an idea," he smiled. "I wouldn't be surprised . . .."

He stopped and pointed at the lights in the distance. Eindhoven is headquarters for Phillips, one of the largest electronic firms in the world. Their products range from cassette players to electronic microscopes. Under the brand-name "Norelco" they supply a major part of television transmission equipment and their records are played all over the world, But they started as a manufacturer of light bulbs. The Dutch, sometimes mockingly, call Eindhoven "The City of Lights". Of course, it did not compare to Paris, or even the lights of Broadway, but Eindhoven did seem to show more lights at night than most other Dutch cities.

"We're almost there," said Vledder.

"You know where it is?"

"Yes, in the outskirts of town, on this side."

Shortly thereafter they stopped in front of a somber, long, three-story building. There were still lights showing behind a number of windows. Obviously some people were still awake.

Stiffly, the two cops alighted from the car and walked toward the huge, oak door. Vledder pulled on the bell and they heard the sound from inside the bowels of the building. It took several minutes before a light came on over the door, the door opened and an older gentleman appeared in the opening. He looked with surprise at the two men.

DeKok lifted his hat and said:

"We're from the police. We just came from Amsterdam." Both Vledder and DeKok showed their badges. "We're here in connection with the assault on little Andrew Bearburgh."

"From Amsterdam . . . at this hour?"

DeKok nodded resolutely.

"We would like to talk to Andrew a moment . . . it's important."

The man hesitated, looked from Vledder to DeKok and back again.

"I don't know," he said slowly. "My wife is with him at the moment. The boy just won't sleep. He has a fever, is restless. He keeps calling for his father. My wife and I, we're not sure what to do. The doctor left about an hour ago, a delivery, he'll be back later, he said, but . . ." his voice trailed off, the man sounded concerned. "You know," he went on, "that it was his father who . . ."

"Just so," said DeKok. "That's exactly why it's so important we speak to the boy. It seems incredible. We know Mr. Bearburgh."

The man made an undecided gesture.

"But it seems to be true. The other boys confirm it."

"Other boys?"

The man sighed tiredly.

"It's all been related to the police already," he said with annoyance. "There were six of them. They were on their way to the Pool, a recreation area a few blocks away. They go every

201

Wednesday. They have a big swimming pool there . . . with a wave-maker. It happened on the way to the Pool."

DeKok smiled patiently.

"Still," he insisted, "I would like to talk to him."

The man finally shrugged his shoulders, opened the door wider and allowed them inside. Then he closed it carefully. He led the way down the long corridor and nearly at the end of the corridor they climbed two sets of creaking staircases. At the top the man motioned them to wait.

"I'll call my wife," he announced.

He shuffled away and came back with a small woman who stepped resolutely toward the policemen.

"Can you identify yourself?" she asked abruptly.

Vledder and DeKok repeated the process of showing their badges.

"You're right," DeKok said with a winning smile. "It pays to be careful. It's not at all impossible that the murderer may come back."

She looked at him sharply.

"But his own father?"

"Do you believe it was his father?"

She hesitated for a moment.

"It seems that way," she admitted.

DeKok leaned toward her.

"Mrs. . . .eh?"

". . . Gevaert."

"Mrs Gevaert, before you and I . . . before we all, make a terrible mistake . . ."

* * *

Young Andrew Bearburgh looked pale. A small, pitiful, intensely pale face with a large bandage covering the left cheek and part of the forehead peeked from above the sheets. The boy had bright blue eyes and the same luxurious blond hair as his mother. He lifted his head painfully from the pillows, but when he saw who entered he dropped back with a disappointed look on his face. DeKok approached carefully and placed his hat at the foot-end of the bed. He grimaced, rubbed his nose, scratched the back of neck, looking for an opening. He tried standard phrases.

"My name is DeKok, DeKok with kay-oh-kay. Not the French way, *Cocque*, you are studying French, aren't you? But the Dutch way *Kok* which means Chef, or Cook, as you know. My great-great-grandfather must have made it *the* cook, a special chef, you see." He realized he was babbling. He always had difficulty with the pain and hurt of children. His heart went out to them. He shrugged his shoulders sheepishly. "May I sit down a moment?" he asked.

A slight flickering of the bright eyes was the only response. DeKok pulled a chair closer and sat down.

"I'm a policeman," continued DeKok. "Earlier tonight I heard you had been in an accident and were in bed. Therefore I came all the way from Amsterdam to have a little chat with you."

"Why isn't my father here?"

"Your father will be here . . . tomorrow."

The boy looked suspiciously at the craggy face of the Inspector.

"Promise?"

DeKok stretched out a large, rough hand. A narrow, pale arm emerged slowly from under the blankets.

"That's a solemn promise," said DeKok seriously. "If he doesn't want to come, I'll bring him myself." Then, noticing the shadow on the boy's face, he laughed heartily and added: "But I'm sure he's very eager to come see you."

"Where is he now?"

"I think he's in the police station in Amsterdam. They were going to pick him up."

"Why?"

"I wanted to have a talk with him . . . as I'm having a talk with you."

"Are you keeping him in . . . in a cell?"

DeKok looked at him candidly.

"Should I?" he asked softly.

Little Andrew blinked his eyes, bravely fighting the tears.

"You must ask him why he did it." It sounded indignant.

DeKok sighed deeply.

"I'll ask him, I promise. But . . . maybe he has forgotten."

Some color came into the pale cheeks.

"Of course, he'll remember. He saw me. He came driving up and I waved at him."

"How did you know it was your father?"

A look of disgust at the stupidity of adults came into the boy's eyes.

"His car, of course. My father drives an Opel GT, one of the latest models, light-blue. It's a cool car. Fast as a race-car. My friends think it's a cool car too."

"Did you see the license tag?"

"No, but it was Father's car."

DeKok pursed his lips.

"You ran into the road and waved?"

Little Andrew turned his head away, toward the wall. His lips quivered.

"I . . . eh . . . I thought he would stop," he stammered. "I thought he wanted to come with us . . . to the pool . . . that he was going to give us a ride. But suddenly . . . suddenly he drove at me . . . he drove *straight* at me. I called Papa . . . Papa, I called . . . and then I fell." He sobbed and licked away a tear that slid down his face. "I thought that maybe he stepped on the wrong brake by accident . . . that he would stop down the road . . . but he drove away . . . he drove away." He now cried freely. "He drove away . . . he didn't even stop to look at me . . . to see what happened."

DeKok swallowed a lump in his throat. Awkwardly, he stroked the blond hair of the child and felt the sweat on the surprisingly cool brow.

"My friends say he's rotten man . . . a rotten father . . . a crazy father who wants to kill me." He turned his tearstained face toward DeKok. "Do I have a rotten father?"

DeKok shook his head emphatically. His craggy face no longer looked tired. He looked serious and the boy seemed to take comfort from the calm face.

"You do *not* have a rotten father, Andrew" he said convincingly. "Not at all. It wasn't your father, this afternoon."

The boy looked at him, holding his breath, a tense desire in his eyes.

"Not my father? But it was his car!"

DeKok smiled.

"How many VWs are there on the road, Fords, Fiats, Chevrolets? You probably know a lot more about cars than I do."

A happy gleam came into the boy's eyes. His mother must have had the same startling eyes, thought DeKok.

"It was another Opel . . . yes, another blue Opel." It sounded jubilant. "With some other guy . . . a stupid man . . . who didn't know how to drive." A smile broke through the teary face. "A stupid man," he repeated, relieved. "Of course, a stupid man who didn't know how to drive." He looked at the Inspector. "Will you tell my friends?"

DeKok cocked his head at the boy.

"They're asleep," he answered. "I don't think there will be time. I still have to get back to Amsterdam. But your father can tell them, tomorrow."

The boy released a long, satisfied sigh.

"Yes," he said with a happy, calm smile on his face. "Yes, he'll do that. For sure."

20

They drove back to Amsterdam at a more sedate pace. Vledder hummed an old school song and DeKok, as usual, was sprawled in the seat next to him, his hat over his eyes.

"I told Andrew it wasn't his father."

"Rather precipitous," Vledder responded, unable to resist the opportunity.

DeKok growled.

"I couldn't care less. I wasn't about to leave that child with the burden of not knowing. Just think what the poor little guy has had to endure already. First the divorce, then the sudden death of his mother and grandmother and now this. It was enough, I thought, I couldn't leave it." He pushed his decrepit felt hat back with a brusque gesture. "And," he continued, "if it turns out, after all, that it *was* his father, I'm ready to personally break every bone in his body."

Vledder looked in surprise at his old mentor. He had seldom heard such a savage tone in DeKok's mouth.

"Andrew Bearburgh *does* have a light-blue Opel."

DeKok nodded, calmer.

"It confused the boy." He straightened himself suddenly, again angry. "How can anybody do such a thing?" he asked furiously. "That attempt on the boy was devilish. The perpetrator could almost expect the boy to approach the car without the least amount of suspicion."

Vledder thought for a while before he spoke.

"There are a number of considerations," he said finally.

"Considerations?"

"Yes. The driver had to know that little Andrew was in boarding school in Eindhoven and he knew that the boy went to the *Pool* on Wednesday's. The attack required some preparation. Time and place were carefully selected." He paused. "While you were with the boy, I contacted the local police. The sergeant was still there. He had done the original investigation and he was working on the situation sketch. According to the State Police it's a marvel that the boy survived. The sergeant also seemed to have trouble believing that it could have been the boy's father. But the facts left him no choice. He had to put through the request for an arrest."

"I understand that, there was no other way. Did you tell him there might be some delay with the arrest?"

Vledder nodded.

"He could live with that. He didn't want to mess up our investigations into the other murders. But he did wonder about something . . . if it wasn't Andrew Bearburgh, how come it was his car?"

DeKok shook his head.

"Nobody got the license plate. It was a light-blue Opel, with retractable headlights and all that sort of stuff. A remarkable car, but not unique. The kid approached it impulsively. But I don't think it really was Bearburgh's car."

Vledder stole a glance at his partner.

"You don't *want* to believe it, that's the trouble."

DeKok nodded slowly to himself and grunted something.

"What?"

"Maybe," said DeKok, "maybe the suffering of that innocent little boy has clouded my judgment." He paused, pushed his lower lip forward. "Tomorrow, later today, find out from the importer how many of those light-blue cars have been imported and what dealers bought them. Then check with the dealers about the buyers."

Vledder groaned inwardly. Maybe Dijk could help.

"And another thing," said DeKok.

"Yes?"

"Get me a picture of Jonathan Weer."

* * *

Robert Antoine Dijk looked tired when Vledder and DeKok entered the detective room at the Warmoes Street station upon their return from Eindhoven. Andrew Bearburgh, nervously smoking a cigarette, was seated next to Dijk. He sprang up when he saw DeKok and walked toward him.

"What's the idea, keeping me half the night?"

"Have you been arrested?"

Dijk motioned in the negative behind Andrew's back. Bearburgh, who could not see the signal, continued in a furious manner.

"I've been enticed, yes enticed, to come here. Supposedly in order to cooperate voluntarily with the police."

DeKok shrugged his shoulders as if he did not understand the problem.

"So, why didn't you leave?" Then, dropping all pretense, he smiled and added: "Of course, in that case I'm afraid that my colleague *would* have arrested you formally."

Bearburgh looked confused.

"Arrested?"

"Yes," agreed DeKok. "Why didn't you tell us you had a son?"

"You never asked me."

DeKok grimaced.

"Come, come. We had a long conversation about your marriage to Juliette. It's obvious that you had plenty of opportunity to tell me that a son had been the result of that union."

"I . . . I didn't think it was important," tried Bearburgh.

DeKok looked quizzical.

"Really?" he mocked. "You didn't think that the inheritance of a portion of the Weer fortune was an important detail? Or hadn't you realized that, because of Juliette's death, as legal guardian of your minor son, you have been manoeuvred into a very important position. You hadn't thought about that?" DeKok's voice shifted from mockery to sarcasm. "Jealousy was *one* of the reasons, but you had a *number* of reasons to wish Juliette's death."

Andrew Bearburgh paled, he licked his dry lips.

"I didn't kill her. I told you that before."

DeKok sighed dramatically.

"You have said that before," he repeated slowly. "Where were you this afternoon?"

"At home."

"And your car?"

"My car?"

"Yes, the Opel."

Andrew looked confused again.

"I took it into the shop, this morning." He pointed at Vledder. "I was here this morning to collect Juliette's things. From here I took the car to the shop and they took me home with a courtesy car."

"What's wrong with your car?"

"Nothing, it was time for maintenance, oil, grease and they were going to adjust the timing. The car will be ready in the morning, later today, I mean." he added, with a glance at the clock.

"The car has been in the shop all afternoon?"

Bearburgh shrugged his shoulders.

"Unless they took it for a test-drive, or whatever." He looked a question at DeKok. "Has something happened?"

"Sit down," said DeKok. Bearburgh sat down and DeKok pulled up a chair for himself.

"This afternoon," DeKok began slowly, "your son was hit by a car in Eindhoven." He raised a restraining hand. "Nothing too serious, happily, but the car that hit him was a light-blue Opel, same year and model as yours."

Andrew fell back in his chair. His face turned gray and distraught.

"My boy . . . hit by a car. How is he?"

DeKok shook his head soothingly.

"As I told you, nothing too serious. Bumps and bruises, a broken leg, no complications. If I were you I'd visit him tomorrow. It'll do him good. He's expecting you."

Slowly Bearburgh rose from his chair. A strange, frightening expression on his face. He looked at DeKok with wide eyes.

"And you thought . . . you thought that I . . ." He grimaced and released a short, raw laughter. "You thought that I . . . my son . . . my own son . . . you're crazy!" His voice rose, broke, wildly he repeated himself. "You're crazy . . . you're just plain crazy!"

DeKok motioned toward Dijk.

"Take the gentleman home," he said listlessly.

* * *

DeKok grimaced at his own reflection in the mirror and pulled his tie straight. He felt like facing the world again. A good night's rest had banished the hellish pain in his calves and had revived his sagging spirit. The tiredness had vanished and the fighting spirits again coursed through his body. He joked with his wife, slurped his coffee with relish and overindulged in large quantities of toast, butter and marmalade. Later, much later than his unpunctual habit, he left the house and strolled leisurely toward the police station.

Vledder approached him cheerfully when he arrived in the detective room.

"They found the sports car!" he exclaimed, happily animated. "They found it not far from the railroad station in Utrecht, in a dead-end street."

"What sports car?"

Vledder looked confused, then realized that DeKok truly did not know the difference between one type of vehicle and another. A car was a car was a car, according to DeKok, and they generally only differed in color and shape. But sedans, coupes, hard-tops, soft-tops, whatever, it was all Greek to DeKok.

"The light-blue Opel that was used in the assault in Eindhoven," explained Vledder. "It isn't Bearburgh's car. I checked already and yesterday his car never left the garage all day."

"All right," answered DeKok, "but why should it be the car they found?"

Vledder smiled mysteriously.

"It's a brand-new car. It still had dealer plates and they were deliberately obscured. The mileage on the car is roughly equal to twice the distance Utrecht-Eindhoven. The car has already been searched for fingerprints, but none were found, not even a fragment. You see, just as with Juliette and the old lady."

"Our careful killer," said DeKok grimly.

Vledder nodded agreement.

"We checked back immediately, of course, and traced the car to a dealer in Utrecht."

"You talked to them?"

"Oh, yes. He knew at once what I was talking about. He had already been contacted by the Utrecht police. The dealer let me talk to a salesman and he told me that a gentleman had come into the showroom around noon, yesterday and inquired after a light-blue Opel of the type we know. It so happened that they had just one on hand in the desired color."

DeKok's eyes narrowed.

"And the gentleman wanted to buy it?"

"Exactly. But there were problems, the car had not been prepared and a few things had to be done. Dealer-preparation, you understand?"

"But they gave in," concluded DeKok, ignoring Vledder's allusion to his ignorance about cars.

"Oh, yes. The car was prepared post-haste. The gentleman was paying cash. All formalities were waived, they let him keep the dealer tags until his own tags would come through. The paperwork was finished by the time the car was ready to roll."

"He gave a name, I assume?"

"Yes . . . Jonathan Weer."

They remained silent. DeKok's cheerful mood had vanished. He had the paralyzing feeling that he was banging his head against an invisible wall. That he would never be able to lay his hands on the killer. But it had better happen soon. Time was running out. The man became bolder by the minute.

He had taken all necessary steps to protect the life of little Andrew Bearburgh, but how long would he be able to keep the safety measures in place. He could not provide protection indefinitely. Only a little while ago, on his way to the office, he had contemplated using the child as bait, but almost immediately, horrified at his own thoughts, he had rejected the possibility as out of the question. He was not going to use a child as bait. There had to be another way, a better way.

"Did we get a decent description, this time?" he asked Vledder.

Vledder looked down-hearted.

"No . . . just as with the antique dealer . . . almost nothing. He was wearing dark glasses, the description is just about as helpful."

DeKok grinned an unpleasant grin.

"A gentleman." It sounded like a curse.

"Yes, a gentleman," repeated Vledder mockingly. "But it's strange. Everybody who knows him and everybody who comes in contact with him, uses the same word: *gentleman*! I guess we can assume he's a charming man who makes a good impression on men and women alike."

"You have a picture yet?" asked DeKok pensively.

"Dijk is on his way with that."

"Where did he get it?"

"From Margo."

"She actually allowed him in the house?"

"Apparently. I sent him over there with the fur coat. He just called in. It wasn't her coat, either. But . . . she did have a photo, as long as we promise to return it."

"Of course," agreed DeKok absent-mindedly.

Vledder looked at him searchingly.

"What do you want with the photo?"

DeKok pushed his lower lip forward in an aggressive gesture. Somehow it changed his craggy features of a good natured boxer to those of a determined bulldog.

"Tonight, after the news, I want it on all channels. We can't wait any longer. We *have* to find Jonathan Weer."

21

The Commissaris looked friendly. He waved in the direction of an easy chair next to his desk. DeKok, a bit stiffly, remained standing. He took the photo of Jonathan Weer from his pocket and placed it on the desk so that the Commissaris could look at it.

"I would like to have this face on the television, tonight, along with a request for further information."

The Commissaris picked up the photo and looked at it closer.

"Who is it?"

"Jonathan Weer."

The police chief dropped the photo as if it was a hot potato. With the tips of his fingers he pushed the picture back toward DeKok and shook his head vehemently.

"Out of the question."

DeKok tapped the picture with a stubby index finger.

"This man is suspected of having committed two murders," he asserted with quiet insistence. "And it seems that his urge to kill has in no way abated. Yesterday afternoon an attempt was made on the life of little Andrew Bearburgh, Juliette's son. We can wait no longer. The man *must* be apprehended as soon as possible."

The Commissaris raised both hands in protest.

"You must do what you have to do, DeKok," he said sharply, implacable, "but this picture will not appear on television."

Apparently resigned with the situation, DeKok retrieved the photo and put it back in his pocket.

"You refuse your permission?" he asked formally, but there was a threatening undertone in the calm words.

The Commissaris looked up at him and raised a cautioning finger toward his subordinate.

"I warn you . . . be careful about what appears in the press."

DeKok seemed unruffled.

"You don't need to warn me. I know my responsibilities. But . . . I *do* have a warning for you." His face became expressionless, cold, distant. Then he added: "If something happens to little Juliette's son, I will personally call *you* to account."

The Commissaris rose, anger flashed in his eyes and his face was turning red. He searched for words. DeKok looked at him and shook his head.

"You don't have to send me away," he said, still with that icy, calm voice, "I'll leave."

* * *

Vledder looked downcast.

"Now what?" he asked.

DeKok rubbed his face, as if trying to bring it alive. On his way back from his chief's office he had clamped his jaws together so hard that it hurt.

"Only a miracle can help us now," he said despondently. "I had hoped to bring some new life into the investigation by showing Jonathan's photo on TV. To help the miracle along, so

216

to speak. But the old man flatly refuses. To be honest, I was afraid he would refuse."

"You have any other suggestions?"

DeKok shrugged his shoulders.

"Yes, posters in the Post Office, the usual. But it seldom does any good. It's not dynamic, it doesn't grab people. And even if you do get results that way, it takes too long." He scratched the back of his neck in a familiar gesture. "Did you make copies of the picture?"

"Yes, some. I asked for glossies and they'll be ready this afternoon. They gave the original back almost right-a-way. I still have it. Why?"

"What happened to Dijk?"

"He's doing the rounds with the fur coat again," smiled Vledder.

"Did he get inside at Margo's?"

"Yes, but nothing out of the extraordinary. Of course, he was unable to do a thorough search, but it was his impression that Margo was alone. Jonathan wasn't staying with her, if that's what you mean."

"Uhuh ... about Margo. Did you check on the intended marriage between her and Jonathan, in Edam?"

"Yes," Vledder said wearily. "Of course, almost immediately after you asked me to do so. And everything checked. They have registered their intention to get married, but a definite date wasn't set." He opened a drawer and started to rummage nervously. "But, now that you mention it, there *was* something strange. I'm trying to remember. I made a note of it ... let me see ..."

"Try your notebook," suggested DeKok drily.

"What? Oh, yes, of course." Vledder took out his ubiquitous notebook and flipped through the pages. "Yes," he said, "here it is. The address ..."

"What address?"

"Jonathan's."

"So?"

"Well, I always thought that Jonathan had no regular address and if he did, it would be in Amsterdam. But not so. In Edam he gave Ermelo as an address. 191 Heatheredge Road, Ermelo."

DeKok stared thoughtfully into the distance.

"Ermelo . . ." he said slowly, "Ermelo . . . isn't that where they have that large Psychiatric Hospital?"

"So what?"

DeKok did not answer. He walked over to the coat rack and retrieved his old, decrepit, felt hat.

"We're going to see Margo," he announced.

"What for?"

DeKok turned around. There was a dazed look in his eyes. It worried Vledder.

"Keep a promise . . . return the photo."

* * *

Margo stood in front of them in the door-opening, beautiful, exciting, tempting, challenging. She wore tight leather pants and a frilly, transparent blouse that concealed nothing. Her hands were on her hips and her glorious hair was held away from her face by a black, velvet head-band. Her hips were slightly thrust forward and she gave such an impression of sexual enticement that DeKok's puritanical soul blushed down to the tips of his toes. Outwardly, however, he remained impassively unaffected.

After they had stated their intentions, she turned around without a word and seemed to float down the corridor as she led the way to a large, comfortable living room. An immense, sectional leather sofa enclosed three sides of the space in front of an open hearth made out of unhewn flagstones. Tasteful paintings decorated the walls.

"A nice room," admired DeKok. "It has atmosphere."

Margo smiled, gestured around.

"A present from Jonathan," she said airily. "But, gentlemen, please sit down. Make yourself at home." She indicated the comfortable sofa. When the Inspectors had seated themselves, she took her place across from them and pulled her knees up under her chin. She placed her arms around her pulled-up legs and added: "Jonathan is a generous lover."

DeKok's eyebrows threatened to jump across the room. Margo held her breath, her mouth half open. She was momentarily mesmerized, as were most people who were suddenly confronted with the uncanny phenomenon.

"Lover?" asked DeKok as his eyebrows subsided.

Margo recovered herself, only half believing that she had seen what she thought she had seen. She looked mockingly at the gray sleuth.

"Yes, lover . . . a dirty word, Mr. DeKok?"

"I was under the impression that the two of you were getting married."

The mocking look left her eyes, she seemed to shrink slightly within herself.

"Marry . . . as long as you keep him away from me . . . how can I marry? Jonathan is no fool. He'll know that you're keeping this house under surveillance."

DeKok pursed his lips.

"The two of you could flee, elope. You don't *have* to get married in Edam."

She lowered her legs and stared at the floor.

"I haven't heard from him at all. He doesn't write, doesn't call, nothing . . ."

DeKok looked at her searchingly. He heard the tone of sorrow, of disappointment.

"What's with Heatheredge Road in Ermelo?"

She looked at him,

"Where did you get that information?"

"It was on the marriage application."

She pouted.

"An old villa. We needed papers, identification, for the application and then it turned out that Jonathan was still registered as living in Ermelo."

"Still?"

"Yes. He was born in Ermelo. The villa is owned by the Weers. The family used to use it as a summerhouse, when the children were smaller."

"And now . . . who lives there now?"

"According to Jonathan it hasn't been used for years."

"Have you ever been there?"

"About two months ago. Jonathan wanted us to live there, eventually. He was going to ask his mother to have the property registered in his name."

"And?"

"The place looked neglected, dark and somber. I didn't think too much of it. But Jonathan claimed it was a friendly house with many happy memories."

"Did you restore it?"

She shook her head sadly.

"We never got that far. The house could not immediately be made available. There were some difficulties with the family, I think. Jonathan never really discussed it."

DeKok looked at her evenly.

"Did they object to the marriage?"

She started to cry, softly, pathetically.

"The clique . . . the clique didn't like me. The old woman didn't even want to see me." She sobbed, tears ran down her cheeks. "When Jonathan and I went to visit her, she made me wait outside. Only Jonathan was allowed to come into the house."

"What about the others?"

"I never met them."

DeKok chewed his lower lip, trying to find the words. A certain delicacy made him hesitate, but the question had to be asked.

"Tell me, Margo," he asked diffidently, "are you pregnant?"

She looked at him with a teary face. The hair was plastered to her cheeks and her hands shook. Suddenly, despite the provocative clothing, she was little more than a miserable, helpless, frightened child.

"Are you pregnant?" DeKok repeated gently.

Her nod was barely perceptible.

"We love each other," she apologized. "Truly. You must believe that."

"I believe you."

She sighed. There was relief as well as anxiety in the sound.

"If Jonathan has done anything, he has done it for me, because of me, you see. To get back at them because they didn't want . . ." She did not complete the sentence but stretched out her hand to him in a beseeching gesture. "He has to come back, Mr. DeKok, Jonathan has to come back . . . for me . . . for . . . for him . . . for the . . . for everything."

DeKok looked at her with a sad, compassionate look in his eyes.

"He should come back, Margo, he really should come back." Slowly he rose and placed a tender, soothing hand on her shoulder. "Poor thing," he said solemnly, more to himself than

221

anybody, "poor child, I'm afraid the end of your sorrow is nowhere in sight."

* * *

Vledder aimed the police VW through the heavy traffic of the inner city. A mild smile played around his lips.

"I feel for her," he said, shaking his head in sympathy. "What's she going to do with the child if Jonathan has to go to jail?"

"In a nursery, what else?" growled DeKok ferociously.

Vledder looked at him in surprise. Apparently DeKok was not in a good mood. His usually so friendly face looked like a thundercloud just before the storm broke. With a sad, knowing smile Vledder returned his attention to the road. He knew that mood as well. DeKok struggled with the anger of his helplessness, his inability to do something constructive. He was often difficult to live with at such moments.

Calmly he drove on until they found themselves stuck in bumper-to-bumper traffic. A truck was unloading something and blocked the narrow roadway between the facades of the old-fashioned gable houses and the water's edge. It happened too often to be worthy of comment. Vledder switched off the ignition and prepared to wait.

After a while he turned to DeKok.

"At least the motive seems to become clearer," he began carefully. "Over the years Jonathan's hate toward his family must have grown to an obsession. Last year he was unable to marry Lucienne, then his father died under suspicious circumstances, followed by the machinations of the old lady that effectively blocked him from the company and now, just recently, . . . the trouble with Margo."

222

DeKok did not react. For the first time it seemed to Vledder as if he had not even heard the words, as if the sounds had not reached him. Vledder dropped the subject.

"How is the fuel situation?" asked DeKok suddenly.

"Almost full," answered Vledder, refusing to wonder.

DeKok sighed, straightened out his hat.

"Let's go to Ermelo," he said softly.

22

A large, neglected piece of ground filled with chestnut trees, some birches, wildly growing bushes and a number of scrub-pines. The red of a brick facade and the deeper, wine-red of glazed roof tiles were visible between the many shades of green as the two inspectors approached the entrance to 191 Heatheredge Road.

The path was overgrown, moss grew between the gravel and dead branches snapped underfoot. The house itself looked friendly enough from the outside. It was shaped like a Saxon farmhouse, low, with small windows and a high roof. They walked around the building, slowly, carefully. The house was obviously deserted. All doors were closed and dirty remnants of lace curtains competed with spider webs in front of the windows.

DeKok produced the apparatus that had so often allowed him access through locked doors.

"What do you hope to find here?" whispered Vledder.

"Jonathan."

"You really believe he's hiding out here?"

DeKok looked up.

"I don't know," he said mysteriously, "if you could call it *hiding out*."

"What do you mean?"

DeKok did not answer. The lock had yielded and he pushed open the door. The rusty hinges screeched in protest. Both policemen listened for the least sound but when there was no response from inside the house, they stepped through the door opening. A dank, clammy smell greeted them.

The door led into a mud-room. An old, rusty bicycle rack was mounted on one of the walls, next to a boiler from the ancient heating system. The room was devoid of any other items, or furniture. With careful attention to every detail, they explored the rest of the house. Where possible, DeKok opened windows and brushed aside the curtains and spider webs, allowing some light into the gloomy interior.

"It doesn't look like anybody has been here for ages," remarked Vledder. "Everything seems to be just as dirty and dusty as the rest. At the very least we would have seen some pots and pans in the kitchen. Empty cans, something. A person has to eat. Even the toilets are dusty."

"Dead men don't eat," said DeKok in a morbid voice.

Vledder smiled denigratingly.

"A macabre joke," he said.

DeKok looked grim.

"It wasn't meant as a joke." His tone matched the expression on his face.

He turned abruptly and stepped out of the bedroom into the long corridor. The diffused light from small, smoked-glass windows in the front-door at the end penetrated almost halfway down the corridor. Vledder followed close behind, an uncomprehending look on his face.

Suddenly DeKok stopped.

"The floor of the corridor," he pointed out. "It's been swept."

Vledder looked over his shoulder.

"Where?"

226

"In front, near the door. It's clearly visible from this angle. There's a lot less dust." He bent down for a low-angle view. "As far as I can see, it's from the first door on the right to the front-door."

"Vledder knelt down beside him.

"You're right. From what must be the living room to the front. We haven't been there, yet."

Slowly they proceeded down the corridor. They stopped in front of the indicated door. Vledder kicked and slowly the door fanned open. They looked into a large, rectangular room. Little light penetrated through the small windows and the room was almost dark. DeKok walked over to the windows and pulled the curtains down from the rusty rods. It made a lot of difference. With his back to the window he let his gaze travel around the room. Three over-stuffed chairs with the stuffing emerging from between the seams, were arranged on an old, gray carpet. A small, round table completed the furnishings. Everything was dusty, but nothing compared to the layers of dust in the other rooms.

DeKok noticed a spot on the carpet, near one of the chairs that seemed less dirty than the surrounding area. He came closer and lowered himself onto one knee. After a while he rose with some difficulty and shook his head.

"I'm afraid it's too old," he said bleakly. "probably useless for our purposes."

"What?"

"Blood . . . or what's left of it."

Vledder frowned.

"What could have happened?"

DeKok gestured impatiently, refusing to indulge in idle speculation.

"Did you check all the closets and cupboards?"

"Yes, there weren't many. You saw most of them in the kitchen."

DeKok consulted his watch.

"Then we'll have to look outside. We have plenty of time left." He pointed toward the driveway. "On the way here, we passed a hardware store. Go and get a couple of shovels."

"Shovels?"

"Yes, to dig with."

Vledder became obstinate. His face turned red and a determined look came into his eyes. Sometimes DeKok's cryptic remarks and actions were just too much for the impulsive young man.

"I'm not getting anything," he said sharply, "unless you tell me exactly what we're doing here."

DeKok sighed. It had seemed so obvious to him.

"Searching . . . searching for a corpse."

"A corpse?"

"Yes, Jonathan's corpse."

* * *

They drove back at a ridiculously low speed over the long dike that separated the "old" land from the "new" land. Cars bulleted past them in the left lane. To the right a red, glowing sun sank slowly behind the horizon that was formed by yet another dike, the dike that separated the "polder" from the remaining water of the former Zuyder Zee. DeKok was driving and from time to time he looked with genuine concern at his young colleague. Vledder looked pale. His face still showed traces of horror and astonishment.

"How do you feel?"

Vledder took a deep breath.

"I was nauseated, but it's passing."

"You told them to keep it out of the press."

"Yes, they promised." He was referring to the State Police. "I don't think the Sergeant wanted any publicity himself. But, of course, he can't control that."

"Where did they take the corpse?"

"To Utrecht. Dr. Rusteloos will meet it there. He said there were facilities at the Academic Hospital for a police autopsy." Vledder gagged as he said the last word.

Vledder had attended many autopsies and seen many corpses in his young career. Usually he was able to hide his reaction behind a cool, calm, almost heartless exterior. But this time, with just DeKok for company, he had lost his self-control. This latest corpse had affected him more than others. Perhaps it was because there was no audience for which he had to "look tough." DeKok indulged him. He had seen colleagues with three times as much service as young Vledder who still got sick at the sight of a dead body. As long as he gets sick, thought DeKok, he has still retained his humanity. Too many cops became callous in the job. DeKok firmly believed that as one became callous about dead bodies, one became callous about administering the Law, the rights of people as individuals.

Vledder manfully tried to continue the conversation.

"Do you have any idea how he died?"

DeKok shrugged his shoulders, the VW responded accordingly. Hastily DeKok adjusted his steering.

"It's difficult to say," he said after the car was again, more or less, under control. "I suspect by stabbing, a dagger, a long knife and then internal bleeding. I'll wait for Dr. Rusteloos. He'll find out for sure."

Vledder pulled out a handkerchief and wiped his face. He was still pale.

"I guess we'll have to arrange for an official identification."

DeKok nodded agreement.

"No question about it. We must have an official identification. But I don't expect any surprises. It's Jonathan Weer, without a doubt. His wallet was still in his pocket, including his money. Only the passport was missing." He sighed deeply. "And if we want to be absolutely sure, Interpol can arrange for the Paris fingerprints."

"How long has he been there, you think?"

"At least four weeks."

"Four weeks?" there was disbelief in Vledder's voice.

"Just about."

Vledder swallowed.

"But . . . but in that case . . . in that case he could never have committed the murders."

"*That*," said DeKok to the windshield, "is an accurate observation."

* * *

Vledder stopped the car in front of the massive office building of Chemical Industry Holland. Before they entered the city, by mutual consent, Vledder had resumed his driving duties. Now he looked up through the windshield. All the lights in the building were still on.

"Five departments are working overtime," explained DeKok. "Cleaning crews are busy in the rest of the building."

"Are you sure he's here?"

DeKok nodded.

"He has to be here. He hasn't left the building, according to reports. And the reports are right," he added, pointing across the parking lot. "His car is still here."

They entered the marble entrance hall through an unlocked side door. Their path was blocked by a self-important, authoritarian person in the uniform of a guard.

"Where do you think you're going?" he asked in a bullying tone of voice.

DeKok smiled thinly.

"We're inspectors," he lied, "of the cleaning company. There have been some complaints and we're here to check up."

"Oh." The man seemed to enjoy the thought that someone was going to be in trouble.

DeKok raised his hat and walked toward the elevators.

"We'll find our way," he tossed over his shoulder.

They entered the elevator and were lifted to the third floor.

"You know where to go?"

"Very precisely."

Vledder looked at him with barely controlled tension.

"You've been here before?"

DeKok shook his head as the elevator doors opened.

"I've been well informed, that's all."

They exited the elevator and walked over thick carpets, past decoratively illuminated flower pots toward an imposing, leather-padded door. DeKok hesitated for a moment, then he opened the door and, followed by Vledder, stepped inside.

The office was the size of a small ballroom. A large, wide desk stood against the far wall. The distance from the door to the desk was long and offered the man behind the desk plenty of time to observe his visitors.

Count on DeKok to do the unexpected, thought Vledder. DeKok had pushed his hat far back on his head and approached the desk in a nonchalant, careless manner, like a *bon-vivant* on the way to one more drink before calling it a night. But every sinew and muscle in his body was under severe stress. The man at the far end of the room was extremely dangerous and capable of anything. He had already tried to kill four people and succeeded three times. The fourth had barely escaped his homicidal rage.

DeKok ambled on in his typical, somewhat waddling gait while Vledder tried to blend in the background. DeKok stopped in front of the desk and stretched out his hand. Automatically, without thinking, the other reached across and shook hands. DeKok held the other's hand in his own while he looked evenly at the man. Vledder sidled, almost unobserved, toward the side of the desk.

"I wanted to express my regrets," said DeKok. "My condolences on the death of your brother."

DeKok saw the man's pupils contract, a tic pulsated on his cheek. The hand, which he still held in his grip, pulled to free itself. From the corners of his eyes DeKok watched Vledder complete his circuit of the desk. Vledder loomed up behind the suspect. DeKok released the hand.

The man's face was red. He swallowed. His eyes flickered angrily.

"What's the meaning of this?" he raged.

DeKok straightened his hat.

"Jerome Weer . . . you're under arrest."

23

They were gathered in the cozy living room of DeKok's house. DeKok looked with pleasure on the two young detectives who had joined him. Dijk and Vledder were comfortably sprawled in easy chairs.

Mrs. DeKok was, as ever, the superb hostess, providing innumerable delicacies and an unlimited supply of delicious coffee. But first DeKok poured generous measures of an extremely fine cognac into the waiting snifters. He was just vain enough, and human enough, to enjoy the admiration of the younger men.

Dijk was the first to break the silence after they had all sipped from their cognac with the proper reverence for such a noble product of the distillers art.

"What am I to do with that idiotic fur coat?" he asked. "The thing is giving me nightmares. I'll be happy to be rid of it."

DeKok smiled.

"Give it back to the owner," he advised.

"And who might that be?"

"Young Mrs. Weer."

"Jerome's wife?"

DeKok nodded.

"She may not want to wear it anymore, but it's hers."

Vledder demanded attention.

"How did you know it was Jerome?" He asked urgently. "How did you know that the corpse of Jonathan . . ."

DeKok raised a hand, stopping the flow of questions.

"Have another sip from your cognac," he advised laughingly, "and I'll try to explain."

He picked up his own glass and rocked it gently in his hand.

"What fascinated me almost from the beginning," he began, "was the dualistic nature of the killer . . . a strange, contradictory behavior for which, at first, I could find no reasonable explanation. Perhaps that sounds complicated, or convoluted, but it isn't."

He inhaled deeply from the heady aroma that rose from his glass. He took a long sip and placed the glass on a small table next to his chair.

"Cast your mind back," he continued, "to the first murder . . . Juliette's murder. The purse was carefully cleaned and Kruger, our best fingerprint expert, couldn't find a trace of a print. The killer had been very, very careful. So far so good. But then, after making sure that all traces have been obliterated . . . he does something stupid. I mean, what sort of murderer pulls, totally unnecessarily, an easily recognized medallion from around the neck of his victim and then takes it to an antique dealer the very next day and . . . identifies himself with his own passport?"

There was silence. Vledder and Dijk looked at each other. Dijk shrugged his shoulders, as if attempting to answer the question, but Vledder admitted that he had not thought about it.

"You're right," he said, "it *is* contradictory. Stupid . . . of me, I mean. I can't believe I missed it."

DeKok made a feeble gesture.

"The same sort of contradiction is encountered during the assault on little Andrew. The killer carefully obscures the license plates, cleans the car thoroughly before abandoning it and then, when he buys the car, for cash, mind you, he again identifies himself with his own name." DeKok paused. "The conclusion," he went on, "was obviously one of two possibilities: either Jonathan Weer was a dangerous schizophrenic who alternated between being a charming *gentleman* and a homicidal maniac, or . . . Jonathan Weer was *not* the killer. I was more and more convinced of the latter as the case progressed."

Vledder looked surprised.

"But you issued an APB for him!"

"Yes. But I had no other choice." DeKok sounded indignant. "All indications *did* point toward Jonathan. And that's all I had to go on. The facts. The rest was nothing but theory, nebulous theory at that. But . . . in either case, it was a matter of some importance to find Jonathan as soon as possible."

It was Dijk's turn to look confused.

"But why? If he wasn't the killer?"

DeKok explained:

"Jonathan was the only one to deny the suspicions against him and thereby shed some light on who the *real* killer might be. That's also why I asked Vledder to arrange for the sensational newspaper articles."

Vledder nodded his understanding.

"You wanted to blackmail him in coming forth."

DeKok raked his hands through his hair.

"Yes, at the time I didn't know, needless to say, that Jonathan had already been killed."

A depressed silence fell on the gathering. The thoughts about the sad end of Jonathan occupied all. Then Vledder leaned forward.

"When did you first suspect that Jonathan wasn't alive anymore?"

DeKok delicately sipped his cognac.

"After the minimal return on the newspaper articles and, above all, because of Margo Stover. You see, *all* reports described him as a friendly, thoughtful, charming *gentleman* and it seemed a bit incredible to me that he would leave that girl, that young woman, no matter what the circumstances, that he would leave her without any word about his whereabouts for more than four weeks. After all, she was his intended and . . . as was later confirmed, she was pregnant." He rubbed his face with a tired gesture and drained the last of his drink from the glass. "It may sound strange, but Margo's pregnancy actually hastened Jonathan's death."

Mrs. DeKok looked surprised.

"But why?" she asked. "What possible connection could there be?"

The old sleuth hesitated for just a moment. He glanced at the bottle, but decided to wait.

"We'll touch upon the motives in a moment, but first we have to go a little bit further back in history. We have to go back to the death of old Henry Weer."

Dijk looked alert.

"It *was* murder?" he asked tensely.

DeKok nodded dejectedly.

"Yes, the first in the series."

"Jerome?"

"No, not Jerome."

"Who, then?"

"Old lady Weer, his wife."

Vledder looked at him with disbelief.

"She poisoned him?"

DeKok rubbed the bridge of his nose with a little finger and seemed to reflect on what he was about to say.

"That's to say," he hesitated, "in a way. Henry was addicted to morphine as a result of his treatment for gallstones. Old Dr.

Gelder prescribed morphine as needed. Jonathan would routinely have the prescriptions filled and, if necessary, would take care of additional supplies, above and beyond what was prescribed. Henry did not inject himself, but trusted his wife to take care of that." He paused. "From here on in, it's pure speculation," he continued after a while. "Jerome, who, by the way, has made a complete confession, refused to discuss his mother. But he *knew* that she was responsible for the death of his father. And he *knew* that she had done it in order to make sure that he, Jerome, would become the heir-apparent at CIH."

Mrs. DeKok waved impatiently.

"How did she do it?"

"Insulin."

Vledder's face cleared as if he had just discovered a new revelation.

"The ampules we found in the villa."

Dijk did not understand.

"But," he interrupted, "I thought that insulin was a medicine."

"Yes," answered DeKok, "a very beneficial medicine *if* you need it to cure, or control a certain condition, such as diabetes. But when administered to someone who *doesn't* need it, and when administered in small doses, over a period of time, it becomes a deadly poison."

"Is that what she did?"

"What?"

"Administer small doses over a period of time?"

DeKok stared thoughtfully into the distance.

"Yes, it took some time, but she mixed the insulin with the morphine and slowly poisoned his system in more ways than one. If she had administered a lethal dose all at once, he might have gone into a coma and the risk of discovery would have been greater. If anybody were to find him in that state, such as A/B

Opperman, they would almost immediately think about poisoning. But the way she did it, in small doses, it was almost undetectable. Henry would require more and more morphine, that's all, because the doses he did receive were weakened by the insulin."

Vledder nodded understanding.

"And that just gave her more opportunities to administer the insulin."

"Yes," said DeKok thoughtfully, "that's exactly what happened. While his body screamed for the morphine he needed, the poison levels were steadily increased. He must have been in unbearable pain at times. It was almost to be expected that Opperman immediately suspected foul play."

"My God," said Mrs. DeKok, aghast. "The poor man: gallstones, morphine withdrawal and insulin poisoning. It's a wonder he survived as long as he did. What a cruel, heartless thing to do. What a . . . what a . . . *snake*!"

DeKok smiled at his wife's spontaneous indignation.

"You're not the only one to call her that. Old Mrs. Weer was indeed the malevolent influence in that family. A capable woman, highly intelligent . . . but cold-blooded, cunning and merciless. Her observation that Jerome was the only one of her children remotely like her, is a telling remark in that context."

They remained silent. DeKok, with a sigh of relieved anticipation, lifted the bottle and poured another round. The cheerful ritual was unable to banish the serious expression from the faces watching him.

"All right," Dijk said impatiently. "We understand the role of the old lady. But what about the rest?"

DeKok sank back in his chair, holding his glass up against the light.

"Jonathan figured out what had happened aboard *Julia*. 'They killed the old man,' he said later. And, when they were all gathered around the deathbed, he swore vengeance."

"The oath on the *Julia*," smiled Vledder.

"It was a theatrical gesture . . . no more. Jonathan simply wasn't the type to be an avenger. But he was smart enough to realize that he should keep away from the murderous duo: mother and son."

Mrs. DeKok shook her head in despair.

"But why didn't he?"

DeKok smiled sadly.

"Margo. Margo and the house in Ermelo. Jonathan wanted to get married, but his mother objected. Jonathan made it clear to her that he was old and wise enough to do as he wanted and that he was serious this time. Margo was pregnant and he wasn't about to abandon her."

"What about an abortion?"

"No, that wasn't Jonathan's way. He was old-fashioned in that respect. He had caused her to be 'in the family way' and he was prepared to do 'the right thing'. Also . . . he truly loved her."

"So?"

"Margo and Jonathan registered to be married. Then it became high time that something happened. Under the pretence of having to evaluate the house in Ermelo, Jerome managed to entice Jonathan to meet him there."

Vledder paled at the recollection.

"And then he killed him and buried him in the garden."

DeKok took a long, thoughtful sip from his favorite beverage.

"Yes," he answered after a long pause. "And that's when Jerome conceived the idea to rid himself of his entire family. If he eliminated all the heirs, one by one, he would be in sole control of CIH. The family owned more than sixty percent of the

239

company and he would not have to share his power with anyone, especially he would no longer have to defer to his mother. His plan was as simple as it was brilliant. Using the oath aboard *Julia* as an excuse, a motive, he would make sure that all clues would point to Jonathan ... a dead Jonathan ... a carefully hidden, dead and buried Jonathan. The police would never find him out."

"Except for DeKok," grinned Dijk.

DeKok raised his arms in protest, careful not to disturb his drink.

"I would never have gotten there without Vledder. He has done a lot of legwork in this case. And so have you," he added with a nod in the direction of Dijk.

Pleased and embarrassed, the two younger men murmured thanks.

"But I have more questions," announced Vledder after a while. "*Where* was Juliette killed?"

"Jerome had enticed her to Jonathan's house in St. John Street. He had told her that they had arrange the paperwork for the house in Ermelo. When she arrived, he told her that Jonathan had had a flat tire and would meet them in Jerome's summer house in Seadike. Unsuspecting, Juliette accompanied her brother and when they came to the house in Seadike, he strangled her. His original plan was to bury her in the sand dunes, but he then realized it would be easier to implicate Jonathan if he deposited the corpse of his sister in Slate Maker Alley. He wrapped the corpse in his wife's fur coat and drove back to the city. He had planned to remove the fur coat."

Everybody looked amazed.

"But ... but why didn't he?" asked Vledder, voicing the thoughts of the others.

DeKok smiled.

"Old Bart had to piss and entered the alley at the wrong time."

Vledder slapped himself on the forehead.

"And he fled *without* the coat."

DeKok sighed.

"Any more questions? I would like another drink and all that," he pointed at the platters of delicacies, some of which were placed on little burners to keep them warm, ". . . and that smells delicious."

Vledder stood up and did the honors with the bottle, while Mrs. DeKok busied herself choosing an appetizing selection for her husband.

"Just one more question," said Vledder as he poured the golden liquid into DeKok's glass. "Why did old lady Weer not react when her house was broken into?"

DeKok looked at him.

"Can't you guess? The break-in was faked. Jerome busted the window from *inside* the house, *after* he had killed his mother."

"Of course," commented Vledder sheepishly.

Then everybody became busy filling plates and praising the culinary gifts of Mrs. DeKok. It was as if they wanted to banish all further thoughts of the series of murders.

"Still," said Mrs. DeKok, when she returned with a fresh pot of coffee and a thoughtful expression on her face. "It's really strange," she sounded confused. "All those killings . . . it's just not normal."

DeKok looked up at his wife with a fondness that was heart warming to watch.

"But Jerome *wasn't* normal, my dear. As a child he had been treated in the Psychiatric Institution in Ermelo. I discovered that when I wondered if Jonathan was mentally disturbed. It wasn't Jonathan, but Jerome who was schizophrenic."

24

A slow, lazy drizzle descended from low-hanging clouds. The clouds looked like they were anchored to the tops of the windmills and churches and would never leave, as if Amsterdam was doomed to eternal, unceasing rain.

DeKok pulled up the collar of his raincoat and pressed his hat deeper over his eyes. In his typical, somewhat waddling gait he stepped across the gravel of the old cemetery. Water dripped from his face.

Jonathan Weer was being buried for the second time. Properly this time, with a proper coffin and all the proper rituals with which the dead are honored. DeKok had felt an overwhelming urge to be there. To pay final homage to the man he had never known but who was indelibly engraved in his memory.

The cemetery looked sad and deserted, more so than a cemetery had a right to look. The flowers seemed to have lost all colors and the birds seemed to be sheltering from the rain. As he looked up, he saw a woman in the distance. Lonely and alone she stood under the overhanging roof of the Chapel.

When he came nearer a happy smile of recognition lit up DeKok's face.

"Black Ginny," he exclaimed with genuine admiration in his voice. "How nice you look, gorgeous, all in black."

She smiled sadly.

"I had to buy it special. Our kind of women don't usually own mourning clothes."

A large, gleaming hearse drove up with unseemly haste and braked in front of the Chapel, throwing wet gravel from under the wheels. A man emerged who ran for shelter and then addressed the two of them.

"You're here for Mr. Weer?"

Both nodded in response.

"Oh." The man was visibly disappointed. "You may follow us."

He ran back to the car and the car proceeded at a decorous speed toward the grave. DeKok and Ginny followed on foot. Suddenly DeKok noticed that Ginny was without an umbrella.

"Your nice clothes are getting all wet," he said with concern. "Let me give you my raincoat."

She stopped him by placing a hand on his arm, a sad, cheerless look in her eyes.

"Don't bother," she said resignedly. "After today I'll never have to wear it again." She grinned bitterly. "I haven't even paid for it. I had to borrow the money."

DeKok looked at her in astonishment.

"Then why . . . why did you come? You hardly knew the man."

She looked around.

"Do you see anybody else?"

"No, we're the only ones."

She nodded to herself.

"That's why . . . I had a feeling that nobody would show up . . . that's why I came. I couldn't stand the thought that there would be nobody at the grave." Tears suddenly appeared in her eyes, mixed with the rain as they rolled down her cheeks.

"Poor Jonathan," she sobbed. "Such a beautiful man . . . so rich . . . so many friends . . ." She worried with her handkerchief, wiped her face. "And look who's here . . . look who's taking him to the grave . . . a cop and a whore."

DeKok placed a soothing arm around her shoulders. He suddenly felt a strong bond between them.

"Our Lord sat down with publicans and sinners," he reassured her. "And it is written: *Blessed are they that mourn, for they shall be comforted.*"

About the Author:

Albert Cornelis Baantjer (BAANTJER) first appeared on the American literary scene in September, 1992 with "DeKok and Murder on the Menu". He was a member of the Amsterdam Municipal Police force for more than 38 years and for more than 25 years he worked Homicide out of the ancient police station at 48 Warmoes Street, on the edge of Amsterdam's Red Light District. The average tenure of an officer in "the busiest police station of Europe" is about five years. Baantjer stayed until his retirement.

His appeal in the United States has been instantaneous and praise for his work has been universal. "If there could be another Maigret-like police detective, he might well be Detective-Inspector DeKok of the Amsterdam police," according to *Bruce Cassiday* of the International Association of Crime Writers. "It's easy to understand the appeal of Amsterdam police detective DeKok," writes *Charles Solomon* of the Los Angeles Times. Baantjer has been described as "a Dutch Conan Doyle" (Publishers Weekly) and has been called "a new major voice in crime fiction in America" (*Ray B. Browne*, CLUES: A Journal of Detection).

Perhaps part of the appeal is because much of Baantjer's fiction is based on real-life (or death) situations encountered during his long police career. He writes with the authority of an expert and with the compassion of a person who has seen too much suffering. He's been there.

The critics and the public have been quick to appreciate the charm and the allure of Baantjer's work. Seven "DeKok's" have been used by the (Dutch) Reader's Digest in their series of condensed books (called "Best Books" in Holland). In his native Holland, with a population of less than 15 million people, Baantjer has sold more than 4 million books and according to the Netherlands Library Information Service, a Baantjer/DeKok is checked out of a library more than 700,000 times per year.

A sampling of American reviews suggests that Baantjer may become as popular in English as he is already in Dutch.

Murder in Amsterdam
Baantjer

The two very first "DeKok" stories for the first time in a single volume, containing *DeKok and the Sunday Strangler* and *DeKok and the Corpse on Christmas Eve*.

First American edition of these European
Best-Sellers in a single volume.

ISBN 1 881164 00 4

From critical reviews of **Murder in Amsterdam**:

If there could be another Maigret-like police detective, he might well be Detective-Inspector DeKok of the Amsterdam police. Similarities to Simenon abound in any critical judgement of Baantjer's work (*Bruce Cassiday*, **International Association of Crime Writers**); The two novellas make an irresistible case for the popularity of the Dutch author. DeKok's maverick personality certainly makes him a compassionate judge of other outsiders and an astute analyst of antisocial behavior (*Marilyn Stasio*, **The New York Times Book Review**); Both stories are very easy to take (**Kirkus Reviews**); Inspector DeKok is part Columbo, part Clouseau, part genius, and part imp. Baantjer has managed to create a figure hapless and honorable, bozoesque and brilliant, but most importantly, a body for whom the reader finds compassion (*Steven Rosen*, **West Coast Review of Books**); Readers of this book will understand why the author is so popular in Holland. His DeKok is a complex, fascinating individual (*Ray Browne*, **CLUES: A Journal of Detection**); This first translation of Baantjer's work into English supports the mystery writer's reputation in his native Holland as a Dutch Conan Doyle. His knowledge of esoterica rivals that of Holmes, but Baantjer wisely uses such trivia infrequently, his main interests clearly being detective work, characterization and moral complexity (**Publishers Weekly**);

DeKok and the Somber Nude
Baantjer

The oldest of the four men turned to DeKok: "You're from Homicide?" DeKok nodded. The man wiped the raindrops from his face, bent down and carefully lifted a corner of the canvas. Slowly the head became visible: a severed girl's head. DeKok felt the blood drain from his face. "Is that all you found?" he asked. "A little further," the man answered sadly, "is the rest." Spread out among the dirt and the refuse were the remaining parts of the body: both arms, the long, slender legs, the petite torso. There was no clothing.

First American edition of this European Best-Seller.

ISBN 1 881164 01 2

From critical reviews of **DeKok and the Somber Nude**:

It's easy to understand the appeal of Amsterdam police detective DeKok; he hides his intelligence behind a phlegmatic demeanor, like an old dog that lazes by the fireplace and only shows his teeth when the house is threatened (*Charles Solomon*, **Los Angeles Times**); A complete success. Like most of Baantjer's stories, this one is convoluted and complex (**CLUES: A Journal of Detection**); Baantjer's laconic, rapid-fire storytelling has spun out a surprisingly complex web of mysteries (**Kirkus Reviews**);

DeKok and the Dead Harlequin
Baantjer

Murder, double murder, is committed in a well-known Amsterdam hotel. During a nightly conversation with the murderer DeKok tries everything possible to prevent the murderer from giving himself up to the police. Risking the anger of superiors DeKok disappears in order to prevent the perpetrator from being found. But he is found, thanks to a six-year old girl who causes untold misery for her family by refusing to sleep. A respected citizen, head of an important Accounting Office is deadly serious when he asks for information from the police. He is planning to commit murder. He decides that DeKok, as an expert, is the best possible source to teach him how to commit the perfect crime.

First American edition of this European Best-Seller.

ISBN 1 881164 04 7

From critical reviews of **DeKok and the Dead Harlequin**:

Baantjer's latest mystery finds his hero in fine form. As in Baantjer's earlier works, the issue of moral ambiguity once again plays heavily as DeKok ultimately solves the crimes (**Publishers Weekly**); . . . real clarity and a lot of emotional flexibility (**Scott Meredith Literary Agency**); DeKok has sympathy for the human plight and expresses it eloquently (*Dr. R.B. Browne*, **Bowling Green State University**).

DeKok and the Romantic Murder
Baantjer

At first the murder of Sister Georgette seems a mystery. Who could possibly benefit from killing this nurse, so respected and appreciated by all. Marten is arrested on the night of the murder during an attempted burglary on a bank. His finger prints have been found in the home of Sister Georgette. Naturally he is suspected of the murder. Marten denies the allegation but confesses that he received a letter from the nurse with the request to visit her.

First American edition of this European Best-Seller.

ISBN 1 881164 08 X

From critical reviews of **DeKok and the Romantic Murder**:

A clever false-suspicion story. Everyone should read these stories (**CLUES: A Journal of Detection**); for those of you already familiar with this loveable old curmudgeon, you're sure to enjoy this installment. Score one for the Dutch; their beloved detective promises to hang around for quite a while (*Dorothy Sinclair*, **Rapport**).

DeKok and Murder on the Menu
Baantjer

On the back of a menu from the Amsterdam Hotel-Restaurant *De Poort van Eden* (Eden's Gate) is found the complete, signed confession of a murder. The perpetrator confesses to the killing of a named blackmailer. Inspector DeKok (Amsterdam Municipal Police, Homicide) and his assistant, Vledder, gain possession of the menu. They remember the unsolved murder of a man whose corpse, with three bullet holes in the chest, was found floating in the waters of the Prince's Canal. A year-old case which was almost immediately turned over to the Narcotics Division. At the time it was considered to be just one more gang-related incident. DeKok and Vledder follow the trail of the menu and soon more victims are found and DeKok and Vledder are in deadly danger themselves. Although the murder was committed in Amsterdam, the case brings them to Rotterdam and other, well-known Dutch cities such as Edam and Maastricht.

First American edition of this European Best-Seller.

ISBN 1 881164 31 4

From critical reviews of **DeKok and Murder on the Menu**:

One of the most successful achievements. DeKok has an excellent sense of humor and grim irony (**CLUES: A Journal of Detection**); Terrific on-duty scenes and dialogue, realistic detective work and the allure of Netherlands locations (**The Book Reader**).